Runaway Cowboy

JUDY CHRISTENBERRY

D0625489

MILLS & BOON®

Pure reading pleasure™

LIBRARIES NI	
C700003155	
RONDO	11/03/2009
F	£ 3.19

First published in Great Britain 2009
by Harlequin Mills & Boon Limited,
Eton House, 18-24 Paradise Road, Richmond, Surrey TW9 1SR

© Judy Christenberry 2008

ISBN: 978 0 263 87035 0

23-0409

Harlequin Mills & Boon policy is to use papers that are
natural, renewable and recyclable products and made from
wood grown in sustainable forests. The logging and
manufacturing processes conform to the legal environmental
regulations of the country of origin.

Printed and bound in Spain
by Litografia Rosés S.A., Barcelona

JUDY CHRISTENBERRY

has been writing romances for more than eighteen years because she loves happy endings as much as her readers do. A former French teacher, Judy now devotes herself to writing full time. She hopes readers have as much fun with her stories as she does. She spends her spare time reading, watching her favourite sports teams and keeping track of her two daughters. Judy lives in Texas. You can find out more about Judy and her books at www.judychristenberry.com.

Chapter One

James Bradford stepped out of his black Mercedes and surveyed the Lazy L. The dude ranch was nestled in a lush valley, beneath the majestic Rocky Mountains near Steamboat Springs, Colorado. Through his expensive shades, he could see the corral in the distance. He could also hear the happy laughter of people. He took a deep breath of clear, crisp air.

"Not bad," he muttered. Now he just had to see if the offer of work was still good. The ranch's owner, Cliff Ledbetter, had offered him the job because Cliff was old friends with Jim's uncle. Jim had met Cliff several times. But he was interested in the job because he wanted out of his current position as a stockbroker working on Wall Street. He'd made a lot of money, but not enough to buy and set up a ranch of his own.

He could get back to the life he wanted by coming here.

He entered the large house that looked to be the main building. Removing his shades as he entered, he immediately spotted a young woman seated behind the counter at a desk.

He could've said "not bad" about her, too, but he didn't want to be rude. "Hello," he said instead.

The dark-haired woman looked up in surprise. "Good morning," she said as she got up. "How may I help you?"

He returned her smile. "I'm looking for Cliff Ledbetter. Is he available?"

"Yes, of course. He's at the corral just behind the house."

"Thanks." He turned to go out the front door.

"It's closer if you go out the back door. Just go down the hall behind the main staircase."

"Thank you. I will." As he walked down the hall, he smiled at the thought of the remarkably beautiful woman in the front office. Getting to know her would be his first priority.

Right after he moved in.

AFTER THE STRANGER HAD walked away, Jessica sat back down at her desk. Who could the man be? Her grandfather didn't have that many callers, other than his friends from the valley, and she knew all of them. Besides, they all dressed in jeans and boots, not in what looked like a custom-tailored designer suit and leather loafers.

The man was more her age than her grandfather's. Not that she was looking for a man right now, good-looking or not.

"Jessie? Where are you?"

She recognized her brother's growl. "I'm at my desk, Pete. What's wrong?"

"This can't be true!" he ranted as he came around the corner.

"What can't be true?"

"This cattle drive you offered the customers!"

"Pete, don't you remember? We talked about it."

"Not this week! We're doing roundup! I can't have a bunch of inexperienced riders wandering around on horseback! It's not safe."

After shuffling papers, Jessica asked, "Is this the only week you can do roundup? Because I have a larger group of guests requesting a cattle drive next week. It's what we do, Pete. Show people how to be a cowboy."

"I don't think we'll be finished by next week."

Jessica covered her face with her hands. Then she looked up. "Pete, this is why we had those meetings when we were planning out the summer season— to schedule certain activities for our paying customers."

"That's not my fault! I had a lot on my mind!"

Jessica was so frustrated with her oldest brother she was tempted to scream. "Pete, you're not thinking! Our reputation will depend on what people say about their time here!"

"Hey, kids, I want you to meet someone," an older voice called out, interrupting their tirade.

Jessica halted the argument mid-stride, but it

wasn't easy. She looked up to see the dark-eyed stranger she'd admired before walking with their grandfather. She managed a smile.

"This is James Bradford. He's going to work here."

Jessica stared at the man, momentarily speechless. Pete obviously wasn't. "He is? You a cowboy?"

"I was at one time. Going to be again," the man said.

Jessica finally found her voice. "Granddad, what do you mean?"

"Jim is Tony's nephew. He'll be great."

"Who's Tony?" Jessica asked. She didn't mean to be rude, but she needed the facts.

"He's the guy I go fishing with down in Texas. Remember? We were in the navy together."

Holding her smile in place when she wanted to scream, she nodded at the man. Pete just stood there stone-faced.

"What are you good at?" Pete asked, still eyeing him.

James Bradford remained silent.

Both Pete and Jessica stared at their grandfather.

"You're not going to like this, but I hired Jim to run the ranch. You all will report to him," Cliff Ledbetter said.

Dead silence filled the room. Then both Pete and Jessica started to protest, loudly, to their grandfather.

Mr. Bradford raised a hand and calmly said, "May I suggest we take this discussion somewhere that the guests can't overhear?"

Guiltily, Jessica looked around. He was right, of

course, but she didn't like a stranger pointing out the obvious.

"Let's go to the kitchen," she said.

She knew their chef, Mary Jo, who had gone to school with her, would be in her room. They had a window of about an hour before lunch preparations began.

Abandoning her desk, Jessica marched toward the kitchen, listening to the purposeful footsteps that followed her.

When she could stand it no more, she whirled around and faced her grandfather. "Granddad, how could you do this?"

"I did it for you, child," her grandfather said, but before Pete could complain, he added, "and for your brothers."

"But, Granddad, we have it all arranged," Jessica said, even as a hundred different problems that had come up in the past few months popped into her head.

"And is everything working out?"

"Well, not exactly, but—"

"Hell, no, it's not working!" Pete answered.

Before she could question him, she heard her name being screamed in the hallway.

She swallowed. Great. Another temper to deal with!

"We're in the kitchen, Hank," she called out to her middle brother.

"I can't believe you—" Hank abruptly halted, his mouth still open, when he realized she wasn't alone. "What's going on here?"

"Granddad just hired this *dude* to be our boss," Pete said precisely, leaving no doubt to his opinion.

Mr. Bradford stepped up. "Look, this is the reason your grandfather hired me. He said the three of you are always arguing about everything. That must be hard on all of you. But if I'm the bad guy, then you won't have to fight among yourselves."

"But—but you're a dude!" Hank complained, using the phrase that described their non-cowboy guests. People who knew nothing about cattle or horses.

"Give me a few minutes to change, and at least I won't look like one," Jim said with a crooked grin.

Jessica found herself captivated by that grin. Then she shook her head, trying to rid herself of the thought.

"You don't think I can pull it off?" he asked, catching her smile.

"No, I wasn't— I mean, I was thinking of something else." She hoped she didn't blush.

"We got one of the bedrooms in the back hallway still empty, don't we, Jessie?" her grandfather asked.

"Yes, but—"

"Good. Come on, Jim. I'll show you where to put your stuff."

"My bags are still in my car, Cliff."

"Where are your keys? The boys can bring them in."

"Why don't I go grab everything and change clothes. Then I'll see what I can do to put out some fires."

"Good, good, that will be great," Cliff said, nodding while he proclaimed his approval.

As soon as Jim left, the battle ensued. Both of her brothers were yelling at her, her grandfather was yelling at her brothers, and Jessica just gave up.

They were all still mourning the sudden deaths of their parents six months ago in a car accident. After the shock had worn off, they'd made plans to keep on with the cattle operation, while continuing to run a working ranch, but to add a dude ranch to bring in extra income. They had all thought the Lazy L had a better chance of surviving when the price of beef went down as it sometimes did. But the stress of the transition was wearing on all of them.

Their grandfather actually owned the four-hundred-acre ranch. It had been in the family for three generations. Many years ago, though, he'd moved into town and left his son and his daughter-in-law to run it. When they died, Cliff returned to the ranch to ensure that everything went well.

Only it hadn't.

When Jim returned to the kitchen with his bags, Jessica got up and showed him the way to his bedroom. Anything to get away from her brothers.

"Are you about to cry?" he asked the moment they shut the kitchen door behind them.

"No!" she snapped.

He said nothing till they reached his room. "I'll be out as soon as I change."

Realizing he was waiting for her to go, she marched out of the room, after telling him where the employee bathrooms were.

But she didn't want to go back to the kitchen and fight with her brothers. They were hurting, too, she knew. None of them had taken the time to mourn their parents' deaths.

Ever since that horrible tragedy, the three of them hadn't been able to get along. They had fought constantly the past six months. It amazed her that they had gotten as far as they had.

The door behind her opened and she spun around, surprised to see how much a change of clothes had changed Jim. Before, the man had looked like a Wall Street big shot. Now, in jeans, boots and a western shirt, he looked like a real cowboy. A handsome cowboy, she admitted.

"Let's go," he said, putting his hand on her elbow to guide her back to the kitchen. "I'll try to get this mess sorted out as quickly as possible."

She shrugged off his touch. "Don't think it'll be easy! We're all stubborn."

"No kidding," he muttered.

She looked at him sharply. "What's *that* supposed—"

"Let's just go to the kitchen."

When they entered, Hank and Pete were still arguing. Her grandfather was watching them with a frown.

"Enough already," Jim yelled, so he could be heard over the two of them.

They turned and stared at him.

"Now you look like a cowboy," Pete said.

"Yeah," Hank said, actually agreeing with his brother.

"I've worked as a cowhand and acted as boss on a cattle ranch in Texas. Now, let's get down to business. What problems do you have right now?"

Both brothers started at the same time. Jim lifted his hand again. "One at a time."

"Pete always gets to go first because he's the oldest and that's not fair!" Hank immediately said.

Pete retorted. "Hey, I'm the—"

"This time Hank can go first," Jim said.

Hank gave a nod, satisfied. "Well, we have people who think they're expert riders and they don't even know to mount their horses on the left side! I can't put those people on our best horses!"

"You should have a stable of mostly tame horses that won't get upset if they're mounted on the wrong side. That said, though, you should be directing the riders to mount from the left. Do you?"

"Well, yeah, but I still wouldn't call them great riders," Hank protested.

"No one said you would. But you don't have to be absolutely honest with your customers. What you want to do is find horses that are comfortable around a lot of people."

"Yeah, I got those."

"Good. Let me know if you run into problems."

"Okay."

Jim turned to Pete, who started in immediately.

"*She* expects me to have the guests wandering around when I'm trying to run a roundup!"

Jessica wanted so badly to step into the argument, but she wasn't going to. First she'd wait for Bradford's decision.

"Did you have a meeting to discuss your plans for the next week?" Jim asked Pete.

"Yeah, but I wasn't listening because— Well, just because." Pete's argument sounded lame to Jessica.

Jim turned to her. "Did you explain to your brother what you expected from him?"

"Yes, I did. Specifically."

"What did you promise?"

"We advertised our ranch as a working ranch, meaning we have cowboys and cows. I promised four people they could ride with the cowboys for several days."

"You didn't promise they would be involved in roping and branding?"

"No."

"Pete, could you use the four people to hold the herd as you sort out the ones with calves?"

"I could, but I don't see why I should!"

"Because if I'm in charge, you have to do as I say. I'm not being unreasonable, you know."

"I know, but—"

"Pete!" Cliff Ledbetter said.

"But, Granddad!"

Once again, Cliff's response was only his grandson's name. "Pete!"

"Okay, okay!" Pete exclaimed, and marched out, still irritated.

"Now, for you, Jessica," Jim began.

"I don't have any problems, now that they aren't yelling." She raised her chin, just in case he thought he'd revamp her job, too.

"Actually, I think you do. If you're going to make this a topflight dude ranch, you have to be out there with your guests. You need to hire someone to do the clerical and receptionist duties."

"But I can—"

"I don't think the ranch can succeed with all of you arguing about every little thing," he said gravely.

"But there's no way we'll succeed if the books aren't balanced!" She looked at him, challenging him to disagree with her.

"That's true. But still, someone else could do that while you're being the face of this company. If you're moving among the guests, you'll make them feel important."

"But I don't have anyone to handle my regular job."

"I'm sure we can find someone. I'll supervise that person and make sure everything is running satisfactorily."

Jessica turned to her grandfather, her eyes imploring his help.

But she received the same answer her brothers had. "Jessie, you have to do what Jim says. If you don't, then this idea will ruin all of you. That's why I hired him to come take charge. To save you."

"Oh, Granddad," Jessica said with a sigh.

"Go on, Jessie, go mingle with the guests," Cliff said.

She walked out of the kitchen just as Mary Jo walked in.

"Hello," she said, and batted her lashes at the stranger.

"Mary Jo, here is your new boss," Cliff said.

Mary Jo did a double take. "But what about Jessica?"

"He's her new boss, too."

Mary Jo took another look, a measuring one before she stuck out her hand. "Hi, I'm Mary Jo Michaels."

"Hello, I'm Jim Bradford, the new manager. And you're the chef?"

She smiled. "Yes, I am."

"What kind of meals are you serving the guests?"

"Jessica and I plan the menu." She turned to a shelf and pointed out to him a chalkboard menu.

After studying it, he said, "Nice job. Don't you need help to prepare them?"

"Yes," she said, and looked at her watch. "I have four helpers who should arrive in five minutes."

"Good. I'll talk with you later, after I've had lunch," Jim said with a smile.

Mary Jo smiled back. "I've never had any complaints."

"Good. Let me ask you a question. What would be the best way to advertise for someone for the front desk?"

"On the bulletin board at the grocery store in Steamboat."

He nodded. Then he headed toward the desk, the one Jessica had been occupying earlier, followed by Cliff.

"What do you think?" Cliff asked.

"I think you were right."

"Which part?"

"The part where you said they would destroy themselves and the ranch if they continued on as they are."

"I knew it," Cliff agreed with a sigh.

"Don't worry. I think you called me at the right time. And it was the right time for me, too. I've been away from the land for too long."

"Glad to hear it, son. I promised your uncle I'd do right by you, though we can't match the salary you gave up."

"No, I didn't think you could, but I've put back money and made some investments to carry me for a while. Your offer of ten percent of the ranch, as well as a salary, is more than generous."

"Okay. Now what?"

"I'm going to look around. Can you go put up a sign at the grocery store advertising for a receptionist with some bookkeeping skills?"

"Don't need to. I know someone."

"Oh?"

"Yeah, she's a widow and needs the money. Used to work as a bookkeeper a few years ago."

"Great. Call her and then let me know. Here's my cell phone number." He wrote it down and handed the paper to Cliff.

"Thanks, Jim."

Jim enjoyed a nonchalant stroll out to the corral. The pace here was certainly different from his old job on the stock market in New York. And so was the air. He drew in a deep breath.

He climbed up to sit on the top rail and watch some cowboys instruct new riders.

There were several other cowboys sitting on the rail. He introduced himself and asked a few questions, till he heard an unfriendly voice from behind him.

"Are you trying to find out what we're doing wrong?"

He looked over his shoulder and found Jessica Ledbetter standing behind him, her legs apart, her arms akimbo.

"I wondered where you'd gone," he said mildly.

Resentment still on her face, she climbed the rails and slung both legs over them to sit a short distance from him.

"I was just thinking—"

"I bet you were," she said, interrupting him.

"You know, Jessica, things will go better if you don't fight me."

"I may have to do what you say, but that doesn't mean I have to enjoy it."

"But isn't being out in the fresh air preferable to bookkeeping?"

"Sure, if that was all I had to worry about. But spending my day sitting on the rail of the corral won't fix the books!"

"Your grandfather wants to hire a widow he knows."

"Leslie Brown."

"You know her?" he asked, raising an eyebrow.

"Of course I know her. This is a small town. Besides, I think Granddad is in love with her. He wanted me to hire her, but I didn't think we could afford to do that right off. Anyway, Leslie isn't hurting for money. She wouldn't take the job."

"Your grandfather seems to think she will."

Jessica twisted her mouth but didn't say anything.

After a minute he tried again. "Can you show her what she'll need to know to understand your system?"

"Yes," she snapped.

"Hey, Jessica, look at me!" one of the children called out as the horse he was on was being led around the corral.

She smiled and waved back.

Jim looked at her and wondered if she'd ever smile at him the way she smiled at the boy. The grin lit up her face, put a sparkle in her eyes.

He had his answer almost at once as she turned and once again glared at him. He asked, "So you have no problem with Leslie working here?"

"We don't need her if I do the books."

"Don't you realize you are the most important person on the ranch? If you can be out here to recognize problems before they arise, everyone will be happier."

"I was already doing that!"

"You couldn't possibly notice things happening here in the corral while you were working on the books in the big house."

"So what are *you* going to do?" she demanded.

"Basically the same as you. I'm going to look for little problems and try to fix them before they become big problems."

Jessica ground her teeth and looked away from him. She didn't want him to make her life easy. His being here meant she'd failed. She'd pored over their notes, their plans, their hopes. She'd examined every idea or request that had come in. She'd written wonderful letters to their future guests, not just sending them brochures.

And James Bradford thought he was going to waltz in and take over?

She jumped down from the fence. She needed some time on her own. With her head down, she walked from the corral, ignoring his question that followed her.

"Where are you going?"

She didn't answer.

Chapter Two

When the lunch bell rang, Jessica was forced from her room by hunger.

The guests, thirty-six at full capacity, ate at six tables in the large dining room, which was perfect for family-style dining. The cowboys, however, ate in the bunkhouse, along with her grandfather, while she and her two brothers usually had their lunch in the kitchen with the help. There was no need for conversation and none was spoken during those hectic moments. Jessica sat down at the kitchen table, knowing she'd get her food and she wouldn't have to talk to anyone.

At least that was true before her grandfather's protégé made a change. He came into the kitchen and "suggested" that the four of them eat with the guests, one at each table, to be there to entertain and answer questions.

"While we eat?" Hank asked in outrage.

Pete chimed in. "We're working cowboys. We don't do the social thing."

"Then you need to resign your job, Pete. Because the owners of a dude ranch are selling a way of life, not just a pony ride. These people are here because they want a taste of the West. That's what you have to give them."

As much as she hated to agree with him, Jessica had known all along they had to have more contact with their guests. She'd tried, in between the book-keeping and clerical duties. "He's right." She left her seat at the table in the kitchen and walked out into the dining area.

The nearest table had five people at it. She asked if the sixth chair was taken. They told her no, and she sat down. "I'm Jessica, by the way. Some people, like my brothers, call me Jessie, but I prefer Jessica. Are you enjoying your visit?"

They asked polite questions about her life on the ranch, and what her duties were. One woman, the mother of a nine-year-old boy, said, "There's something I wanted to ask. Robbie wanted to sign up for roping lessons, but he can't ride that well yet. Is that okay? And can I come and watch…to be sure he doesn't get hurt?"

"Yes, of course. I'm sorry we didn't explain it better in the brochure. Roping lessons for the kids don't involve riding at the same time. We have a fake calf on wheels and the kids practice on him after they learn the basics. Trust me, no one gets hurt!"

The kitchen door opened and two of the lunch servers came out with trays of food. Reluctantly following were her two brothers and grandfather. Cliff was the only one wearing a big smile. Jim came after them.

Apparently he'd given specific instructions to spread out among the tables and to smile at all times.

Jessica ignored him. Her brothers might need a lesson on how to be charming, but she didn't.

"I want to know where we meet the cowboys," a young woman named Penny Abraham asked. "The real cowboys."

"Well, there are four in the room right now. One is a little too old for you," Jessie said with a wink, "but the other three could qualify." Pete was twenty-nine, Hank twenty-seven, and she guessed Jim was thirty. "As you go on rides, you'll come into contact with the cowboys. But be sure to pay attention to what you're doing. We don't want any accidents."

She watched as the woman noted the four new additions to the tables. After centering her attention on Jim Bradford, she said, "I want to meet *him!*"

"I'll be glad to introduce you as soon as lunch is over."

The woman stared at Jim throughout the meal.

Jessica decided she'd discovered a way to occupy Jim's energies. Dealing with romantically inclined female guests should take up most of his time.

"I like the one scowling at the next table," her friend Joyce Pedilla said softly.

Jessica looked over her shoulder to identify which brother the lady was talking about. "Oh, that's my brother Pete. He's in charge of the cattle operation on the ranch."

"So he ropes and brands and everything?"

"Absolutely. And the other cowboy is my brother Hank. He's a horseman. Any riding questions should be directed to him. He'll be able to help you."

"Oh, this is so exciting!"

Jessica could almost agree—but for a different reason. Because she could feel Jim watching her all through lunch. His gaze made her skin heat, her pulse pick up. After only a couple of hours, it amazed her that she was so in tune to him.

After dessert, she was about to escort her table out, when Jim touched her on her shoulder. Surprisingly she hadn't been aware of him for the past few minutes.

"Jessica, could I have a minute of your time before you leave?" he asked softly.

"Of course, but first let me introduce you to Penny Abraham and Joyce Pedilla. They both wanted to meet you and Pete."

He nodded to them. "Nice to meet you, ladies. I'll be checking on activities this afternoon. I hope to see you having fun."

"Oh, you definitely will," Penny said, leaning toward him.

"Good. Jessica?" he said, nodding toward the kitchen.

She said her goodbyes to her table. "Let me know if you need anything."

Then she got up and marched to the kitchen.

Once there, she spun around and snapped, "What do you want?"

"I'm glad you didn't talk to the guests that way," Jim said, his tone mild.

"Is that what you wanted? To quiz me on how I handled my role? I know how to entertain guests, thank you!"

"Would you give me a chance before you bite my head off? No wonder you and your brothers are at one another's throats."

"I didn't mean— I knew you were right about what you said, but…I knew if I spent more time with the guests, it would be like pushing a boulder up a steep hill. So I gave up." Her shoulders slumped in shame.

"Jess, you don't have to do it alone anymore," he whispered.

"You don't understand! This ranch is our baby! And we're doing a good job! We've made mistakes, of course, but—"

"I'm not trying to take it away from you. Cliff just thought you needed some help."

"Which makes me a failure!"

"Woman, would you give me a chance to talk? Look, all I wanted was for you to sit down with Leslie and explain your bookkeeping system. That's all! So can we throw out the dramatics until later?"

She knew her expression was sullen, but it was difficult to smile and be happy when he'd just insulted her. And he had, by calling her concerns "dramatics." They were very real!

With her nose in the air, she looked away from Jim and realized Leslie was sitting quietly by, listening to their conversation. Thank goodness she hadn't said anything about the woman. Not that she had anything to say except that her grandfather had an interest in Leslie. How could he even think of remarrying now, at sixty-four?

"Hello, Leslie. I didn't see you there. Jim says you want the job of bookkeeper and clerk with us?"

"Yes, Jessica, I would, if I can do the job. It would be…very helpful."

"Oh, of course. I understood you were quite— I mean, I didn't think you *needed* a job."

"I'm afraid I do."

Jessica looked at the woman, whose white hair had been cut in a very modern style. She was always nicely dressed.

"Well, come with me, and I'll explain what I've been doing."

Leslie got up and followed Jessica as she went back through the dining room, reminding herself to add another table so they'd all have a seat when the ranch was full to capacity.

It amazed Jessica how quickly Leslie caught on. She didn't even seem fazed by the amount of filing that had piled up. She also understood the importance of writing personal letters to those who inquired about the dude ranch.

In half an hour, Jessica had shown her everything and left her to it. She admitted that it was freeing, knowing that the books would be kept up-to-date. She had been overly busy with all the complaints from her brothers and all the extra jobs she was supposed to do.

"Now what do I do?" she muttered. Slowly, she went out the back door, thinking she would see what was going on in the corral. But Hank was organizing twelve people on horseback to take a ride through the forest. He wasn't going on the ride. One of his men was taking the riders alone.

She didn't think that would be a good idea. "Steve, do you mind if I ride with your group? It's such a beautiful day." With a smile, she waited for him to agree.

Didn't he realize he had to let her go? He hesitated for several moments. "Uh, I guess so, Jessie."

"I'll saddle up right away."

She saddled her favorite ride and swung up, snatching one of the extra hats they had hung in the stable.

"I'm ready, Steve," she said as she rode into the corral. "Are all your riders set to go?"

"Yeah. Okay, follow me!"

Jessica already spotted several guests who would need help to complete the ride. They were the last ones out of the corral and they seemed a little nervous on their mounts.

She was enjoying herself until she spotted Jim watching her as she rode along with the two women on the end. Though she stiffened, she thought she hid her irritation as she continued to talk the two riders through their paces.

The ride was supposed to be two hours long. It was offered on the second day of the guests' week, supposedly after they had participated in an hour-long ride the day before. When she questioned the two ladies about yesterday's ride, she discovered they hadn't participated. This was their first time on a horse.

Another problem she'd need to fix. She'd talk to Steve about not pushing the guests too hard. By the time they got back to the corral, her two riders were dragging, complaining nonstop of aches and bruises.

When they entered the corral, Jessica warned both women to delay their dismount until she got to each one of them. The first woman, Alice, managed to get off, but her legs couldn't hold her for several minutes. Finally she toddled to the gate to wait there for her friend Miranda, holding on to the railing. Miranda simply threw herself into Jessica's arms. Jessica staggered and almost fell until strong arms came around her.

"Easy, Jess," Jim whispered from behind her. "Lean on me."

"Miranda, put your feet on the ground," Jessica ordered. She had no choice but to lean on Jim, and she didn't like it.

When Miranda finally put her feet on the ground, Jessica got her to take baby steps toward her friend's side. Then Jessica turned and politely thanked Jim for his support.

"My pleasure," he assured her. "What happened?"

"Hank had one of his men take the group ride this afternoon. He didn't check to see if they'd taken the hour-long ride yesterday. These ladies were real beginners. They're in a lot of pain. Excuse me."

She walked to the women and asked whether they were staying in the main house or a cabin.

"Main house, second floor, room four," Miranda said, whimpering. "I just don't think I can get up those stairs."

"I know what you mean. But I have a secret potion that, when dumped in a hot bath, can make most of the pain go away. Soak in this stuff and you'll be amazed at the results."

"Will you give it to us?"

"Of course. It has one drawback, however. It smells."

"It does?"

A deep voice from behind her said with a chuckle, "It does."

"Oh, are you going to help us, too?" Alice asked. "I'm afraid Jessica can't handle both of us at once."

"I don't think she can, either. My name is Jim. What's yours?"

The lady giggled and said, "Alice."

"Well, Alice, why don't I help you to your room and then we'll ask Jessica to go find this wonderful secret potion."

Jessica helped Miranda to follow in Jim and Alice's wake, but she wasn't happy. She could've gotten both guests up the stairs and into their room without his assistance.

Her conscience told her she had needed him when

Miranda collapsed in her arms. Without his strong arms shoring her up, she might've fallen on her rear.

But she'd never admit it. Least of all to James Bradford.

JIM CALLED A MEETING for Jessica, Pete, Hank and Cliff that night at ten o'clock. That was after he had insisted the men walk the guests back to their cabins in the dark with bright flashlights.

When Jessica assumed she would also participate, he told her to put on a pot of coffee and they'd have their meeting in the kitchen.

She resented being left out of normal duties, even though she was exhausted. As much as she did today, she didn't know how she'd stayed up-to-date with her bookkeeping.

With the pot of coffee ready and mugs set at each place, Jessica lay her head down on the table and fell asleep.

When Jim came in and saw Sleeping Beauty, he hated waking her up, but he couldn't play favorites. Before he could get to her, Hank came in.

"Sure, she gets to sleep!" he complained loudly, stirring Jessica awake.

"I intended to wake her, Hank, but you did that job for me." Jim picked up the pot and began pouring everyone some coffee.

"I'll make this brief, but I want to be sure you understand that you're expected to eat with the guests and keep a smile on your face. And, talk, too, Hank."

"I'm not good at talking."

"They'll take over for you, if you just act nicely to them," Jim said. "Right, Pete?"

"I guess, but I have more important things to do."

"Tomorrow is the lariat roping lessons. Who do you have to teach that class, Pete?"

"I need all my ropers!"

"Then you teach the class," Jim said calmly.

"No! I'm not— I'll send Mitch."

Jim made a note on his papers. "Hank, the man you put in charge of the afternoon ride didn't make any inquiries about whether the guests had taken the hour-long ride on Monday. There were two ladies who hadn't ridden before. If Jess hadn't gone along, they never would've made it."

Hank shrugged. "I told him. He just forgot."

"You were there helping everyone mount and checking out things for yourself. You could've pulled those two ladies out of the group and made sure they had a short first-day ride. We want people happy. Not in the hospital."

Hank muttered under his breath, but he didn't argue with Jim.

Jessica decided her grandfather must have put the fear of God in those two. Or maybe they just responded better to a man. She hated to admit that about her own brothers.

"Now, tell me the problems you had today," Jim said, sitting down and picking up his coffee mug.

There was dead silence.

"No problems? No complaints?" Jim prodded.

"I suggest we each get one night a week to eat in the kitchen. Having to keep a smile on our faces from sunrise to sunset is difficult," Jessica said.

"Good point. Do you each want to pick your day?"

Hank immediately said, "I pick tomorrow!"

"You did notice that it's for only the evening meal, didn't you, Hank?"

"Not all day?" Hank complained.

"No, not all day. Although it would be beneficial to show up at other times, too. So Hank chooses Wednesday night. Pete?"

"Friday night."

"Okay, you realize your sister didn't mean you could duck out of the evening activity, right, Pete?"

"How am I supposed to have a social life if I'm always working here?"

"Maybe, as we get further along, we'll find ways to give each of you time off for a personal life, but not now."

"I guess I'll take Tuesday evening," Jessica said. Then she thought of another idea she'd had that her brothers had resisted. "What about name tags?"

Jim frowned. "Why name tags?"

So he was opposed to them, too? "So we could learn people's names quicker, and also so we'd know if the guest had been here one week already or was brand new, or had special needs. We have a family of four coming in a couple of weeks and the mother is diabetic."

Jim nodded. "Good idea. Can you handle getting them ready?"

"Of course." She'd have them ready for next Monday's influx of new guests. At least, she hoped so. Or was Jim setting her up to fail?

Wearily, she realized she was too tired to think anymore tonight.

"Cliff, do you have anything to say?" Jim asked.

"Nope, you did a good job, Jim."

"Thanks, Cliff. Okay, let's wrap it up for tonight. Breakfast is served from seven to nine. Find a time to say hello to the guests and spread a little cheer. Good night."

Knowing her brothers and grandfather disliked housekeeping, Jessica immediately began gathering up the coffee mugs. She managed three and then turned to get the other two, almost bumping into Jim. He held the other two mugs in his hands.

"I'll take them," she said brusquely.

"Just because you're the only female of the group doesn't mean you have to do the cleaning up, Jess." He stepped around her and put the two cups in the dishwasher. "Remind me to address that subject in our meeting tomorrow night."

"No, I won't."

"Why not?"

"Because they'll think I was complaining about them not cleaning up after themselves. I've tried that before and I didn't get anywhere. They just laughed and said it was my job."

He leaned against the counter. "What if I bring it up because *I* was struck by the unfairness of it?"

"Fine, but don't use anything I've said as a complaint, because I'm not saying anything!"

"I won't need to. I'll simply tell them to take turns or they'll do without coffee."

"Fine. But it wasn't my idea."

"Definitely not."

She turned to head to her bedroom.

"Oh, Jess, can you wait just a minute?"

"Yes?" she said, knowing her exhaustion was apparent in her voice.

"I wanted to tell you that you did a really good job today."

"What are you talking about?"

"You did a great job at lunch, without my forcing you to do so. You just got up and went out there and did your best to charm the socks off everyone at your table. You were answering questions and dispensing advice all over the place. I heard several guests at your table quoting you as they talked to others. It was a nice job."

"Thank you."

"I particularly wanted you to know that going with the two-hour rider group was great. Did you do it because you realized Steve had too many to take on his own?"

"I thought it could be difficult. I mean, Steve tried, but when you have good riders and a couple of poor ones, it's hard to manage."

"True, but you spotted the problem."

"I—I think I forgot to thank you for keeping me from falling."

"Again, my pleasure."

She felt her cheeks flushing, her throat drying. It was time to get out of there before she did something stupid. "Well, good night," she said, backing up until her behind hit the door. She spun on her boots and scooted out the door to safety.

Jim was even more of a threat when he was being nice.

Chapter Three

Jim joined the early eaters for breakfast the next morning. He wasn't surprised to see both Pete and Hank eating a hasty breakfast.

Jessica came in, and though Jim thought it would've been nice to have breakfast with her, she, as per his instructions, joined a table of guests. She greeted them with a smile.

Lucky them.

One of the guests at his table asked him a question at that moment, and, still distracted, he came up with an answer. "It takes a while to be able to relax on a horse. Most of the cowboys have been riding since they were little kids."

"Did you start riding early?" one of the men asked.

"Yeah. I grew up on a ranch and I first started riding when I was three."

"That soon? Wasn't that a little early?"

"My dad had a pony for me to ride and I only rode when he was there to supervise."

One of the ladies said, "But didn't you ever fall off?"

"Sure. That's part of riding. Won't you excuse me?"

He got up to get seconds on scrambled eggs. An excuse, really. He wanted to get closer to Jessica. As he passed her, he said softly, "Good morning."

He got a response but not a smile. Too bad.

He lingered over coffee. Activities didn't start until eight or nine o'clock, depending on what people chose. Several of the guests sat and visited with him, telling him about things they'd done on the ranch.

When Alice and Miranda came down, he asked them how they were feeling.

"A little sore, but not too bad, after we soaked in Jessica's secret potion," Alice admitted.

"If you want to get better at riding, it would be good to go again today, only not for so long. Either Jessica or I could give you both private lessons."

"Oh, that would be wonderful. What time?"

"How about two?"

"Thank you. We'd love it."

"Good. What are your plans for this morning?"

Miranda gave a small smile. "We signed up to go shopping in Steamboat Springs. We thought that would be more fun than horseback riding."

Jim laughed. "You might be right. Is anyone going with you today?"

"Oh, we don't need someone to take us. We're experts at shopping."

Jim laughed and got up and went to Leslie's area

to check the schedule Jessica had posted there. It appeared Cliff was to drive the small bus to Steamboat Springs.

"What's wrong?" Jessica asked from behind him.

He turned to look at her. "Nothing. I just wanted to see who was scheduled to drive to Steamboat Springs this morning."

"Granddad volunteered. He's a capable driver."

"I'm sure he is. What are you going to do this morning?"

"One of our maids is sick. I'm filling in for her."

"That's your job, too?"

"Someone has to do it."

"Don't you have anyone to call?"

"No. And we can't afford to hire an extra maid."

"Okay." He pushed his sleeves up. "Do you need some help?"

"You? I can't see *you* making up beds and emptying trash cans."

"Why not?"

"You just don't strike me as a housekeeper."

"Give me a chance and you'll find out."

She put out her hand. "You're on."

He shook it. "Where do we start?"

They headed out to the cabins. Jessica walked in front, pushing the supply cart. She was dressed in tight jeans today, and for Jim watching her walk in front of him was a delicious form of torture.

When they reached the first cabin, they worked side by side on the bed, then the bathroom.

They repeated the process until they had finished the four cabins.

"So, what do you think?" Jim asked her on the way back to the main house.

She turned to him. "It kills me to admit it, but you did a great job. I didn't expect you to be so efficient. Thank you. I appreciate the help."

He smiled. "I like working with you."

"Me, too."

As they walked, Jim sensed that the hostility he'd felt from her earlier had dissipated. That, at least, was a step in the right direction. Now he just had to get her to like him.

"What are you going to do now?" he asked when they reached the house.

"I need to put some more time in on the menu for next week."

"You won't serve the same menu every week?"

"Some things, maybe, but we want some variety. Mary Jo has a good repertoire."

"I've certainly been impressed so far."

"Told you she's good."

"Do you always serve dessert?"

"Yes. I believe a well-fed guest is a happy guest."

"Good plan."

"Do you want to join us?"

Her invitation was like music to his ears.

Mary Jo was waiting when they got to the kitchen. When she noticed Jim she gave him a smile. "Are you going to supervise?"

"I think I'll do more listening, since food isn't my area of expertise—except to eat it."

Mary Jo laughed. "It's always good to have an extra ear," she said agreeably.

Jessica wasted no time launching into the ideas she had for the next week. For some reason it bothered her that Mary Jo and Jim seemed so friendly. But she didn't want to analyze why.

After a few more minutes Jim stood up. "Sounds like you've got this taken care of. Now I need to talk to Jessica, if you can excuse us, Mary Jo."

"Sure."

Jessica sent him a worried look. "What do we need to talk about?"

He led her out of the kitchen. "Nothing that serious. I promised Alice and Miranda private riding lessons this afternoon at two. Is that okay with you?"

"Yes, if you want to do that. I certainly don't have you scheduled for anything."

"No, I meant both of us."

Jessica gave him a blank look. "What?"

"I said we would both give them a lesson. That way we could take them out for an easy ride. I think they'd like that."

"I—I guess so, if you promised them."

"I think it'll be great. Two o'clock, okay?"

"All right."

"So what are you going to do now?"

"I thought I'd go see how the children's roping lessons were going."

"I'll go along with you. I'd like to see that class."

"Do you think we should both be in the same place? I mean, aren't we supposed to spread out?"

"We will sometimes, but I think this first week in particular it will be all right."

"Fine. The roping lessons for the kids are out in the pasture near the corral. We can watch from the top of the corral."

"Great."

They walked out the back door and around the corral until they were on the side that looked out on the roping lessons.

They climbed up on the fence and sat on the top row.

Jim watched as Mitch, the cowboy, taught the five boys and one girl the techniques of roping. Then they each tried to rope the fake calf, while two others pushed it around.

"He's good with kids," Jim observed.

"Yes. They're having fun and learning something, too."

"We'll have to congratulate Pete on his choice."

Jessica tried to hide her smile, but he caught sight of it. "You don't think he chose Mitch because he's good with kids?"

"No."

"Then why did he choose him?"

"I don't know for sure, but he probably did something to irritate Pete."

"Well, I think we should have Mitch work with the

kids every time. I think he'd be good at riding lessons for kids, too."

"You'd better tell him instead of Pete. Pete will make it sound like he's being punished."

Jim chuckled. "Good point."

Suddenly they both cheered when the smallest child got his rope around the neck of the fake calf.

The little boy ran over to tell his mother what he'd done.

Jessica smiled. "This is one of those moments you'd like to have a camera ready."

"Hey, that's a great idea."

"What is?"

"Why don't we hire a photographer to take pictures during the week, making sure everyone gets his or her picture taken. Could we do that?"

"I guess. I don't know how much it would cost."

"But you don't have to worry about that now. That's my problem."

"Oh, yes. I forgot!" She jumped down from the fence and strode toward the big house.

"Damn," he muttered under his breath. They'd been getting along just fine today. She'd even said her brothers were behaving better because of him. Then he had to remind her that he'd taken her job away from her.

He climbed down and walked toward the house. It wouldn't be long until lunch. Maybe he could make amends when they gave Alice and Miranda their riding lessons. If she showed.

THE FAMILY WITH THE YOUNG roper ate at the table that Jessica chose for lunch.

"May I join you today?" she asked, nodding to the two empty chairs.

"We'd love for you to," the mother said.

"I'm Jessica. I don't think I've met you before. You must've arrived when I wasn't at the front desk."

"That's right. Your grandfather registered us. But I got your letter when I wrote for information. This sounded like such an interesting place."

"Thank you. I'm glad you're enjoying yourselves."

"Oh, we are. We're having such a good time. Jack, my husband, and our older son rode horses this morning, and Timmy and I stayed here so he could learn to rope a calf. And you saw how he did!"

"Yes, I did. You were great, Timmy."

"I wish I'd seen it," Jack said.

"Well, you would have if you hadn't decided to ride this morning."

Jessica thought it would be good to break up their argument, but she couldn't think of anything to say.

Then someone said, "May I join you?"

Jessica turned to glare at Jim.

"We'd be glad for you to join us," Jack said, relief showing on his face.

"Thanks. We don't have many people here today because of the trip into Steamboat Springs."

"Oh, I wanted to go on that tour this morning, but I wanted to see Timmy rope."

"And he did a great job," Jim said, smiling at the little boy, who beamed back at him.

"I took my older son on the riding lesson this morning," Jack said.

"And what did you think?" Jim asked.

"It was wonderful. The scenery was great, and we saw a bear!"

"You did?" Jim asked with a frown.

"Yeah. He was at the stream, farther up. We didn't come close to him."

"I didn't realize bears were part of the scenery," Jim said to Jessica.

"I'm sure the cowboy leading the ride carried a rifle that he would've used if the bear had gotten too close." Jessica kept her voice calm. "But it must've been exciting to see one."

"Yeah, it was." Then Jack said, "But I'm sorry I missed seeing you rope, Timmy."

"That's okay, Dad," the little boy said, oblivious to his parents' argument.

"We're just glad we can keep everyone happy," Jim said.

"Yeah, and I like the food, too." The older boy had his plate piled high.

"Be sure to save room for dessert," Jessica told him.

"Don't worry. He has an enormous appetite. He plays football," his mother bragged.

"So if we played touch football tonight, you'd be one of the captains?" Jim asked.

The boy lit up. "Sure."

"Unfortunately," Jessica interjected, "we're going to watch a film this evening instead. I hope you'll like it."

"What film are we watching?" Jim asked.

"*Calamity Jane.*"

"What's it about?" the teenager asked.

"It's a movie about a young pioneer woman who thought she could do anything a man could do."

"Ha! As if," the teenager said.

"Careful, son," Jim advised. "Women can be a lot more capable than men, you know." He shot Jessica a smile and a nod.

Another compliment? she thought. If Jim kept this up, her brain might agree with her body and she could be attracted to the new cowboy.

Chapter Four

Jessica arrived at the corral about ten minutes before two, not wanting to keep the two new riders waiting. After choosing the gentle mares the novices should ride, she saddled her horse. Finally she picked one for Jim. He was supposed to be a good rider, so she chose one of her brother's stallions.

Then she saddled the other three horses, finishing right at two o'clock. She led all four into the corral just as the two ladies walked up. Jim was nowhere in sight.

"Oh, you're here already," Alice said.

"But where's Jim? We sort of hoped he'd be the one to give us lessons." Miranda suddenly turned red. "I didn't mean— That is, I'm sure you'll do a great job!"

"It's okay, Miranda. Jim said he would be here. Why don't we get started. Maybe he's just running late."

"Okay. Do you want us to come into the corral?"

"Yes, please."

The two women followed her, but they kept their distance from the horses.

"Alice, this is your mount this afternoon. Come meet Freckles."

"Freckles? That's her name?"

"Yes, because of her unusual marking. She has some Appaloosa blood." Jessica pulled her forward. "Touch her nose. It's very soft."

Alice stuck out one finger. "Won't she try to bite me?"

"Never," Jessica said with a laugh. Then she turned to Miranda. "Here's your ride, Miranda. Come on over and get acquainted."

"I don't see why I need to meet a horse!"

"Because she'll be nice to you," a deep voice said.

Miranda spun around. "Jim! Well, since you put it that way, of course I'll meet her."

Jessica rolled her eyes. When she looked Jim's way, he winked at her. Her lips twitched, but she didn't allow the smile to overtake her face. Instead, she held Miranda's horse and showed her how to pet it.

"How are you doing, Alice?" Jim asked.

"Fine. I've met my horse. Jessica said I could pet her."

"Good. Maybe I'd better meet my horse, too. Right, Jessica?"

"He's right here, Jim. His name is Thunder."

"Is that because he's hard to handle?"

"You said you were an experienced rider, right?"

"Right." He petted the horse, getting to know him. "I think I'm ready to mount. How about you, ladies?"

"Are you sure it's a good idea?" Alice said.

"Yes, I'm sure."

"Will you help me, Jim?" Miranda asked.

"Oh, me, too!" Alice joined in.

Jim exchanged a look with Jessica. "Only this once, ladies. Tomorrow you'll have to learn to climb up by yourself."

Miranda was fairly short and unable to pull herself up. Jim had to give her a small boost.

When he got to Alice, she had been watching. "I put my left foot in the stirrup and then pull myself up?"

"Right. Do you think you can do it?"

"Maybe." She followed his instructions and was the most surprised of all when she ended up in the saddle.

Both Jim and Jessica raved about her efforts. Miranda pouted while her friend beamed.

As Jessica mounted her horse, Buck, and rode around the corral, Jim went through the nonverbal commands the new riders should be able to give their horses.

After about ten minutes, he got in the saddle and led the riders out of the corral. Jessica rode next to Miranda and Jim with Alice, keeping their mounts at a slow pace.

When they got back to the corral half an hour later, both women were riding better but, sore and tired, they were ready to call it quits.

Jessica swung down from the saddle and tied up her horse. Jim followed suit.

Under his breath, he said, "Don't unsaddle yet."

Then he moved forward to help Alice. She did much better today and was able to walk, though with a slight limp. Miranda wanted Jim's help in her dismount, but he encouraged her to try it alone.

Jessica hid her smile. Jim was pleasant to the woman, but he didn't seem interested in encouraging Alice's flirtation.

After the two women went to the house, they each unsaddled a horse and put away the tack. Jessica then moved to her horse, but Jim stopped her. "Let's take a real ride. I'd like to see the property."

Jessica hesitated, then realized that the chance to take a good ride didn't come along that often. She nodded and swung back into the saddle.

They left the corral and nudged their mounts to a faster pace than they'd ridden before. The two of them adjusted to an easy lope.

Aspens covered the land they rode through, blossoming in the spring sunshine. Jessica took the lead when the trail narrowed.

When they came to a mountain stream, Jim called for her to stop.

"What is it?"

"I just wanted to look around for a minute."

"Okay."

"Is this stream still here in the fall?"

"Yes. There are also two larger streams on the property."

"Nice. Do you have any trout fishing?"

"There's some. Not a lot."

"Do you offer fishing lessons?"

"We've talked about it, but I haven't had time to line up an instructor."

"Your grandfather couldn't do it?"

"I was afraid it would be too much for him. There are several fishermen I could contact, though."

"Why don't you write their names down. I'll contact them."

Jessica thought for a minute before she agreed. If he wanted to handle this project, that was all right with her.

"Ready to move on?" she asked.

"Sure. Can we look at the other two streams?"

"One of them, but the other is too far away. It would require a longer ride."

"Okay."

She rode across the shallow stream, Jim following her. When they reached the other side, she took a trail that led to the north.

Jessica found herself enjoying the ride, as well as her time with Jim. They seemed in sync, talking and relishing the silence, in turn. Surprisingly she could feel herself falling for him. He didn't pester her with ridiculous questions, didn't argue about where she wanted to go. Didn't flirt with her.

That surprised her most of all.

Ever since he'd arrived at the Lazy L he'd had an eye on her, so she'd expected him to flirt with her on the ride today. But Jim continued to surprise her.

She pulled up her horse when they reached another

stream. "This is the largest of the streams. Right now, it's at its fullest, since a lot of the snow has melted."

"I still see snow on top of the mountains."

"Yes, but the snow lower down has already gone. We have snow on the top of the mountains most of the year."

"Mountains are new to me. We didn't have any in Texas where I grew up. Not much snow, either. How deep does it get up here?"

"Anywhere from two feet deep to the sky's the limit."

"Have you considered staying open during the winter?"

"We've debated it. The skiing is in full bloom during the winter months and we could put up skiers and bus them to Steamboat. We haven't made a decision on that."

"Why not?"

"We thought we should get our feet wet, be in business awhile before we jump in."

Jim studied her. "Are you for it?"

"Yes, but my brothers aren't."

"Why?"

She sighed. "They wanted October through March off."

"What about October and November off, and March and April? Four months' break seems enough."

"I agree. But I thought it best to wait until they realized having guests wasn't so bad."

He nodded. "Do you think they'd agree with that?"

"No. Not so far. But maybe you'll convince them?" She gave him a hopeful look.

Laughing, Jim said, "I think you're being optimistic, but I'll try. I do think you're right waiting a couple of weeks, at least. How soon would we need to start advertising?"

"June or July."

"Okay, so I need to talk to your brothers by the middle of May in case it takes awhile to convince them."

"I think it will."

"But your grandfather wants this operation to succeed. I think he'll back me on the winter season."

"I hope so. The best selling point is that neither of them would have to do much. If the people are skiers, they'll be gone all day. We could run a bus twice a day, and serve breakfast and dinner."

"Good point. That should convince them."

"We could offer some activities, like cross-country skiing and sleigh rides, too."

"Wouldn't you have a lot of work?"

"Yes, but I think it would be worth it."

He smiled. "I love your enthusiasm. Let's talk again mid-May. Okay?"

"Certainly." She was pleased that he liked another of her ideas. "Are you ready to turn back?" she asked after a moment.

"I guess so, but I almost don't want the afternoon to end. This ride has been fun."

"Yes, it has."

Much to Jessica's surprise, they shared a smile that brought a tingle to her heart. Mustering her self-control, she fought the urge to say so. Instead, she turned her horse and started back to the stables. It was important to hold back. After all, he'd only been here a couple of days.

WHEN THEY RETURNED TO the corral, Hank was waiting for them.

His expression was one Jessica knew well. He was ready to unload on someone. She muttered under her breath, "Hank's on the warpath."

"Where have you been?" Hank demanded.

"Showing Jim some of the property." She wasn't going to hide what she'd been doing.

"Well, you'd better get to the house. Granddad is upset and he wants to talk to you."

"What's the matter?"

"I don't know, but he said for you to hurry."

She dismounted. "Would you unsaddle Buck for me?"

"You're supposed to take care of your own horse," Hank growled.

Jim stepped in. "Since there's an emergency, I think you could help your sister."

"It's not my fault! She screwed up somehow."

Jim turned to her. "I'll take care of your horse, Jessica. I'll come to the house as soon as I finish."

"Thank you, Jim." She ignored her brother's frown and hurried in the back door.

Cliff was hovering over Leslie. When he heard footsteps, however, he turned around, anger on his face.

"Granddad, what's wrong?"

"Where have you been? Leslie couldn't find you and she upset some customers through no fault of her own!"

"I was showing Jim around. What's wrong, Leslie?"

The new clerk's voice sounded nervous. "The Blacks wanted a refund. Since they've been here most of the week, I offered to refund them for the days they wouldn't be here. But they were incensed. I told them you would explain the policy to them."

"I'll go talk to them, but it sounds like you handled it fine, Leslie."

Leslie let out a big sigh.

"Are they in their cabin?" Jessica asked.

"Yes. They said they would be packing while they waited for you."

"Okay, thanks."

She could hear Cliff reassuring Leslie while she walked away. He was obviously concerned about her. And why not? Leslie did a good job.

What could she remember about the Blacks? She'd certainly seen them around. Had something gone wrong?

When she reached their cabin, she rapped on the door.

Someone opened the door at once, as if he'd been waiting.

"Mr. Black? I'm Jessica Ledbetter. May I come in?"

"If you insist."

"I wanted to find out what has gone wrong with your vacation. You haven't expressed any concerns before today."

"We won't be treated this way!" Mr. Black exclaimed.

"What way?"

"My wife was chewed out by some cowhand! He had no business doing that!"

"Perhaps we could sit and talk about this. Where is your wife?"

"She's packing."

"Could you ask her to join us?"

He reluctantly got up and stepped to the bedroom door. When a teary-eyed woman appeared beside him, he escorted her to the couch to sit beside him.

"I'm so sorry you were upset, Mrs. Black. Please tell me what happened."

Her husband started speaking.

Jessica interrupted. "I'm sorry, Mr. Black, but I need your wife to tell me about it."

The woman raised her head. "I—I was riding in a group and my horse started running and I couldn't stop for a couple of minutes, but I tried. He was out of control. And the cowboy leading the ride accused me of ruining his horse!"

"I see." Jessica had a hunch. "Was the cowboy named Hank?"

"Yes, he was. I wouldn't try to run away! I was just riding along. But he yelled at me and told me I wouldn't be riding his horses again! We didn't see any point in staying if that was the case."

"I'm sorry you were upset. I'm afraid Hank thinks more of his horses than he does of people. But he will offer you an apology and that horse will not be included in the rides until he's checked out. You're lucky you were able to stop him so quickly. Now, Leslie is right that we can't return all your money. We've fed you for five days and provided animals for you to ride. I'll be glad to prorate the money for you if you still want to leave."

"I don't think that's fair!" Mr. Black said.

"I'm afraid it's all I can offer, other than an apology from Hank and an assurance you won't be put on that horse again."

Mrs. Black nodded. "If you'll promise that, I think we could stay. Right, Harry?"

"Are you sure, honey? I don't know if that cowboy will offer the apology."

Jessica smiled. "Oh, I can assure you of that, Mr. Black. But the choice is up to you and your wife. I'll leave now and go talk to Hank. You can let us know if you want to leave."

"Thank you," Mrs. Black said. Her husband only grunted his goodbye.

Jessica left the cabin and headed back to the corral. When she saw Jim coming toward her, she waited for him.

"What happened?"

She filled him in on the problem with Hank. "I

think they'll stay," she concluded, "assuming I can convince Hank to apologize."

"I think between the two of us, we can persuade him."

Jessica smiled at Jim. "I was hoping you'd support me."

"A hundred percent. Let's go talk to Hank."

When they got to the barn, Hank was working on tack. The barn was shady after the bright sun, so it took them a minute to locate him.

Jessica started right in on him. "Hank, what horse did Mrs. Black ride today?"

He didn't look up. "Snow White."

"Oh, no. Why did you include Snow White? She's difficult at the best of times," Jessica said.

He put down the tack and shot her an angry look. "She's all right. That lady just let her get out of hand!"

Jim took over. "Did you think her skills were good enough to handle that horse?"

"She said she could ride!" Hank countered.

"I'm sure she can, but not a horse that's difficult. And why didn't you apologize for the horse instead of yelling at her?"

"Because she could've hurt the horse!"

"Did you really think she chose to race away from the group?"

Hank dropped his head again. "No."

"Well, you need to apologize to her. And you need to take Snow White out of the group rides. She's obviously too difficult for most customers."

"I don't see why I have to apologize if they're leaving."

Jessica spoke up. "Because we don't treat our guests like that. And they may finish out the week if you apologize."

"Fine."

Jim picked up on his attitude. "You may need to practice in order to sound sincere, Hank. This is important."

"What cabin are they in?"

"Number six. I'll go with you to make sure you do a good job." Jim kept a steady gaze on Hank.

"I don't see any need for that. I know how to say I'm sorry."

"But I want to apologize, too."

"Fine!" Hank said again, only this time with more emphasis.

When the two men walked toward the cabins, Jessica walked back to the main building. There she heard Cliff still reassuring Leslie.

Jessica stopped beside her desk. "It's nothing for you to worry about, Leslie. I spoke to the Blacks." She filled them in on their talk.

"So, they're going to stay?"

"We don't know yet. Hank and Jim are with them now."

"Jim's doing good, isn't he?" Cliff asked, clearly satisfied with himself.

"I guess," Jessica replied, keeping her personal feelings out of her assessment.

"I appreciate your support, Jessica," Leslie said. "I was afraid you'd let me go."

"Don't be ridiculous. I think you're doing a wonderful job. More important, Jim thinks you are, too."

Cliff looked almost as satisfied as Leslie.

When Jim came in, all three looked at him for more information.

"They're staying. Hank did a good job apologizing. He told her his first thoughts were always for his animals, but he should've thought more about what she experienced. I was proud of him."

"Way to go, Jim!" Cliff exclaimed. "I think the boys will come around. It's just a matter of time."

Jessica bit her bottom lip, wondering if Jim had that much time.

Chapter Five

The week finished with mostly good reviews from their first guests. They left Sunday morning and the new guests started arriving that afternoon. Jessica helped Leslie get them registered and gave out their name tags.

"I think the name tags are a good idea," Leslie said.

"Thanks. I wanted to do them from the start, but my brothers were against them. But Jim agreed."

"He's making a difference, isn't he?"

"Yes," Jessica agreed. "But I still wish we could've worked out our problems without him. It makes me feel like I've failed."

"Oh, Jessie, I don't think you should feel that way. Your grandfather is so proud of you."

Jessica hugged the older woman.

"Here comes another family," Leslie announced. "There are five of them. Do you know who they are?"

"The family of five are the Davidsons." She pulled their name tags as Leslie greeted the family and offered to show them to their cabin. She had one of the cowboys who wanted to earn some extra money carry the bags to their rooms.

"I like Sundays," Jessica said after the family went out. "They all come in so happy to be here, looking forward to their week. It's very uplifting."

"I know. And your brothers get the day off." She laughed. "But don't you think they should help you?"

"I think they need the time off so they won't lose their tempers during the week."

"Maybe so." Leslie sounded doubtful. "Does Jim have the day off?"

"I don't know. We didn't discuss that in our meetings."

As if their talk had conjured him up, Jim appeared beside the front desk. "How's it going, ladies? Need any help?"

As if on cue the front door opened and a new couple came into the building with two large suitcases and a small bag that the woman carried.

Jessica smiled. "Hello. Welcome to the Lazy L ranch."

"Why don't you have someone to carry in the luggage?" the man demanded, his voice harsh.

"We'll certainly help you with your luggage now. May I have your name?"

"Haggard."

"Of course. I have your name tags here. We're asking our guests to wear them at all times. It will help us make you welcome."

The man scowled. His wife didn't seem to have an opinion of her own.

"Let me help you with your bags," Jim said, stepping forward. "Where are they staying, Jess?"

"Cabin two, Jim."

He took the two large bags. "Could you carry the small bag, Mr. Haggard?"

"I guess so," the man agreed reluctantly.

Jim shot Jessica a look. She understood his feeling. This couple could be a problem all week long.

"Do you think there's a chance they'll pass up riding?" she asked Leslie after Jim escorted them away.

"I doubt it."

Jessica sighed. "I think I need to warn Hank."

Just then the bus her grandfather had driven to the Denver airport that morning pulled up.

"Take a deep breath. Granddad just pulled up. We're going to have a lot of guests here at once."

When they finished the last of the arrivals, it was four o'clock. "Leslie, if you want to leave early, I think I can handle anything else that comes up. Thank you for being here today."

"I'm glad to do it, Jessica. It increases my paycheck, you know, getting the extra hours."

"I'm glad. I'm sorry I didn't realize you needed a job. I would've hired you earlier."

"I try not to let people know, but my husband didn't carry much insurance."

"Well, I'm glad Granddad suggested you for the job."

"Me, too."

Jim walked over to tell them they got everyone settled.

"Great." Jessica offered him a smile.

"That looks good," he said, returning her grin.

"What?"

"Your smile."

"I didn't know you— Never mind." Why did he make her so nervous with a simple compliment?

"How about a cup of coffee?"

"I'd love one." She turned to Leslie. "Care to join us?"

"I think I'll go on home. But thanks for asking."

"Of course. We'll see you tomorrow."

She followed Jim to the kitchen.

"I think we'll need to come out to the dining room after we get our coffee," she said. "Mary Jo and her crew will be pretty busy putting together this evening's meal."

"That's fine with me."

After they each got a cup of coffee, they went into the empty dining room and sat down. Jessica sighed as she lifted the cup of coffee to her lips.

"Are you tired?"

"No. I'm ready to start the week. We've got the menu set and everyone's chosen different activities. Oh, I meant to ask you, in Steamboat, they offer bike rides down the manicured slopes. Do you think we should offer that?"

"Do you think anyone would choose that? It sounds pretty dangerous to me."

"Some people consider riding a horse to be dangerous."

"If they did, they wouldn't choose a dude ranch for a vacation."

She grinned. "Probably not."

"Have you done it?"

Another grin. "No way. I've skied down those slopes, but I think a bicycle would get out of control quickly."

"Yeah. I had a few wrecks on my bike as a boy. But I'll have to admit I preferred horses."

"I hope you don't mind my asking, but how did a cowboy end up on Wall Street?"

"Dad wanted me to major in something to take me away from the ranch. It hadn't done well for a number of years and he wanted to sell it. When I graduated with a major in Economics, I got an offer to work for a securities company in New York City."

"I see."

"It sounded exciting. And it was. The money was more than I'd ever considered. But I began to feel crowded in the city. The air wasn't crisp and clean. I didn't get to ride, unless I wanted a pony ride in Central Park," he said with a wry smile.

"Did you tell your parents you were going to leave?"

"Yeah. I told them I had money put away. And Uncle Tony is the one who told me about this position."

"Oh, yes. The infamous Uncle Tony."

"I know your grandfather took you by surprise, but he'd been talking to Uncle Tony for a few weeks about what he could do. And I was glad to get the job."

"Well, you seem to be working out. My brothers are listening to you more than they ever listened to me."

He took a drink of coffee. Then he said, "I think your brothers were planning on wearing you down."

She signed. "I guess so."

"Did I ever tell you that I enjoyed *Calamity Jane?*"

"So you didn't think it was too out of date?"

He shook his head. "I noticed your brothers watched it, too."

"They didn't do it willingly. Granddad had a talk with them."

"It doesn't seem fair, since you're always there. They need an attitude adjustment."

"They'll come around. I hope," she added under her breath.

"How about you? Did you go to college?"

Jessica nodded. "Mom and Dad encouraged all three of us to go. The boys took land management and animal husbandry. I majored in public relations and home economics."

"No wonder you've done such a good job setting things up."

"Thanks."

"I meant to ask you about the overnight trail ride we're doing this week."

"That should be fun. I'd like to go on it, but I'm not sure who will hold down the fort if I go."

"How about Leslie?"

"Do you think she'd mind?"

"I don't think so. We could go with Hank and leave Leslie and Pete in charge while we're gone."

She felt gooseflesh on her arms. "You'd go, too?"

"I'd love to go. I've missed this kind of life so badly. You don't have overnight camping trips in New York City, you know."

She laughed at the thought, trying to forget about spending the night under the stars with Jim. It was more difficult than she thought. Better to keep to business, she told herself.

"I've been meaning to add some new things," Jessica began to say. "I've talked one of the cowboys into playing his guitar and singing one night this week. It won't be around a campfire, but we'll have a fire in the fireplace. And we could have a bingo night. I can pick up prizes in Steamboat."

Jim had ideas, too. "What about running the bus into Steamboat Springs for a night out?"

"Oh, yes, there are a couple of bars with entertainment."

"Maybe we should go check them out."

"I think my brothers could give you an idea of what they offer."

He looked disappointed. "I liked the idea of going myself."

"You can go tonight during movie night. Why don't you take Hank or Pete?"

"I thought maybe you and I could go. I'd rather not have Hank or Pete as a date."

She blinked several times. She hadn't realized he'd been offering to take her. "I—I need to be here tonight," she stuttered. "It's their first night."

Jim gave that some thought. "We could have Leslie stay on bingo night and let your grandfather help her out. That'll work, won't it?" He seemed eager to go with her.

As eager as she was to go with him, if she was truthful. "Sounds like a da—" She stopped herself. "Sounds like a plan."

When the ladies came out to set the tables for the evening meal, Jim stood up. "Maybe we'd better get ready for dinner. Come on. I'll walk you to your room."

Jessica felt as if the atmosphere had suddenly changed. It seemed charged with electricity, an awkwardness.

When he left her at her door, she said, "See you at dinner." Then she slipped into her room, unable to believe how the afternoon had progressed.

One cup of coffee and she now had two dates with Jim Bradford.

JESSICA WAS READY ON TUESDAY to take some guests to Steamboat Springs, where she intended to buy gifts for tonight's Bingo winners.

Just as she was rounding up the shoppers—all women—Jim stepped forward. "I think I'll go with you to pick things out. We have to have gifts that men like, too."

Jessica's eyes widened. "But—but don't you need to keep an eye on everything here?"

"Things will be all right. You don't mind, do you?"

She did. She'd looked forward to a day away from the dark-haired temptation. Instead she said, "No, of course not. We're—we're eating lunch there, too."

"Good. I'll get to see the town. I drove through it the first day, but I didn't take time to look around."

"And I bet you want to ride the bicycle down the mountain," she teased.

"Nope! I don't want to break a leg."

"Me, neither. But I did have several couples asking about it. I told them I'd see what I could do."

"*We'll* see what we can do."

"Okay. Ladies, are you ready? We're boarding our shuttle right outside."

"What shall I do?"

She gave him a smile that made him suspicious. "You can stand by the front door and count the number of passengers."

"Okay, but save me a front-row seat." He walked out the door and took up his position beside the bus.

Just what she needed—him looking over her shoulder. He made her nervous, sensitized, too aware of his masculinity. Taking a deep breath she held the door open for the ladies leaving the main building.

On the drive, Jim sat right behind her. He carried on a conversation with several of the women near him. Jessica could understand that. He was a charming, handsome man. That alone would make him a success at his job. But she couldn't help feeling miffed. Why? she asked herself. She hadn't wanted his attention, right?

She parked the bus in the parking lot of the restaurant where they would eat lunch. "Ladies, it's ten o'clock, so the shops will be open. We'll meet here for lunch at one. Have a good time."

She opened the door and watched as her passengers descended. When they were alone, Jim said, "Ready for our shopping trip?"

"Yes. Where shall we start?"

"You know this town better than I do."

She suggested they check the tourist shops down the main street.

An hour later, they had numerous prizes, including a small leather billfold that men or women could use, key chains, a cowboy hat and several pieces of turquoise jewelry. Jessica was so pleased with their purchases, she bought two or three of some items to be prepared for next week.

When they went into the next store, Jim's eyes lit up. "Now, this is my kind of shop," he said.

"Why do you say that?"

"I think a bullwhip would be a good prize," he replied, hefting one in his hand.

"A bullwhip?"

"Yeah. Guys like to try to make it pop."

"But someone could get hurt."

Jim nodded. "I'll just buy one for myself, then."

Jessica got distracted by a display of pocket watches with an engraving of the Rockies, then after purchasing several, a shelf of western-garbed dolls. "These would be perfect for the women and girls."

"I think we have too many prizes for the women," Jim said, coming up over her shoulder.

When she turned toward him, their faces were only inches apart. "In that case," she managed to say, "you need to pick out something that is all male." The words were dangerous, conjuring up images of the virile man beside her. "Other than a bullwhip."

"Hmm. I did see some sexy underwear. How about that?" He gave her an equally sexy smile.

"No! I definitely don't think so."

He leaned in closer, and she could feel his warm breath on her face as he whispered huskily, "You don't like lacy underwear?"

Chapter Six

Jessica had almost fallen into the intimate web Jim had woven. She caught herself just as she'd teetered. She couldn't believe he'd asked such a question. She'd given him a sharp no and refused to discuss something so personal. He could forget about checking out the bars!

But all the way home, she'd thought about his audacity. She never discussed her underwear with anyone, least of all a man she'd met only days ago.

She'd had one intense affair, when she was in college, until she'd found out Cal was seeing someone else at the same time.

Furious with herself for thinking she was in love, she'd avoided the subject of romance ever since. And she wasn't going to start now. Especially not with Jim.

She pulled up in front of the main ranch building, and after the ladies had all exited the bus, Jim was still sitting behind her.

"You should get out here," she told him. "I've got to go park the bus."

"I'll ride with you. You might like some company on the walk back."

"No, I won't," she retorted.

"I'll ride."

She slammed the door and ground her teeth in protest. After parking near the barn, she got out and waited for him to join her. Then she locked the bus.

"Are you worried about someone breaking in?"

"Yes."

"Do you have much theft out here?"

"No."

"So why do you lock it?"

"Because!"

"But—"

She reeled on him. "Don't ask me any more questions, okay?"

"All right. Can we talk about what's really upsetting you?"

"No!" She headed for the main house.

He caught up with her. "Look, I didn't mean I expected you to show me your underwear. I just thought it was an interesting question."

"I didn't!"

"Why?"

"It's none of your business!"

"Okay. If I offer an apology, will that satisfy you?"

"No!" She picked up her pace.

No matter how fast she walked, he stayed in step with her.

She didn't know how to get rid of him, however,

because they were both loaded down with their purchases.

When they reached the back door, she suggested he
put down his packages and she would get them later.

"No. I'll carry them."

She didn't acknowledge his reply. She simply
stalked to Leslie's desk, where she set down her burden.
He did the same, almost hiding Leslie completely.

"My, what have you bought?" Leslie asked.

"Some gifts for bingo tonight. Do you mind if I
unpack them here? Then I can separate out what I'll
use for tonight and what I'll use later on."

"Oh, of course. I'll help you."

Jessica turned to Jim. "I believe Leslie and I can
handle it from here. Thank you for going with me."
She really didn't want to thank him, but she figured
he'd report her to her grandfather if she didn't show
proper respect.

"I have nothing to do, either, and I want to see how
Leslie likes what we've bought."

"Fine!" When Leslie looked at her, a puzzled
frown on her face, she backtracked. "Why don't you
show her what you bought first."

He took out the bullwhip. "I got this for myself.
Jess was afraid a guest would hurt somebody if he
won one of these."

"I think she might be right."

He looked dismayed. "But she bought some
cheesy pocket watches in place of it."

"They're not cheesy. I know they're inexpensive,

but they make a good souvenir." She took one out and showed it to Leslie.

"I love it!"

Jim grumbled something about being oh-for-two as Jessica gave him a superior look. She showed Leslie the other prizes, including a mechanical bank that played music when money was deposited.

"I gave one of those to my youngest son when he was a boy." Leslie ran her fingers over the bank.

"I didn't know you had children, Leslie," Jim said.

"Yes, I have two sons. They've both finished college and moved away. One is in Denver and the other is in Kansas City."

Jessica thought about the reason her parents had wanted to turn the ranch into a dude ranch with a cattle operation. They'd wanted their children to stay home. "I'm sure you miss them."

"Yes, but I don't want to leave this area, so it's nice that I have a job now."

"Yes, one that demands a lot of your time," Jessica pointed out. "It makes it nice for us."

"And for you, especially," Jim pointed out. "Leslie's freeing you up to do other things."

"Yes, I realize that," she said coolly.

Leslie looked first at Jessica and then Jim. "Are you two unhappy with each other?"

"Yes!" Jessica snapped.

"No!" Jim said at the same time.

Leslie said "Ah," as if that meant something to her.

Jessica began unpacking the decks of cards and

board games she'd picked up, and stored them on an empty shelf behind the reception area. "The guests can play these at night," she said. "The kids will enjoy them."

"And they'll come in handy on a rainy day," Leslie added. "Being cooped up inside all day can get really boring."

"Yeah, I hadn't thought of that."

Jim gave a mock look of horror. "Something you didn't think of? Who could believe it?"

Jessica shot him a look and, saying nothing, picked up her prizes and stalked off.

"What did you do, Jim?" Leslie asked after she was out of earshot.

"Gave into temptation."

Leslie's eyes got huge. "Excuse me?"

"I asked her if she wore lacy underwear."

"Shame on you, Jim!" But when she looked at him, he noticed Leslie's eyes twinkled.

LAST NIGHT, JESSICA HAD HAD Darrell, one of the cowboys, sing to the guests. Darrell was a born entertainer and everyone enjoyed it. Tonight she and Leslie would lead the bingo game. Her brothers could be excused and Jim could… She didn't care where Jim went as long as he didn't hang around!

She'd thought her brothers would be pleased when she'd told them that they didn't need to hang around the guests that night. Hank, however, had found several single women that he wanted to spend time with. If they wanted to play bingo, then he would, too.

Pete growled, "Why couldn't I have had some notice? I could've made a date. If I call anyone now, they'll think I'm being rude."

"Hey, Pete, I'll share. I have two ladies. Come sit with us," Hank offered.

"I might as well," Pete continued in his hangdog attitude.

Jessica didn't say anything. If the ladies liked being growled at, he would be a big hit that evening.

"Yeah, we can both eat dinner with them and still obey old high-and-mighty Jim's rules. We'll get there early and save places for them. How about that?"

"Fine with me."

Jessica checked her watch. "Guests start coming down early, so you've got about half an hour, if you want to shower and smell nice."

"We'd better hurry."

Her brothers raced to their rooms, and she went to shower, too. When she came into the kitchen half an hour later, she saw Mary Jo had everything under control. "Did my brothers run through here?"

"Yes. Why?"

"They're saving seats for two single women."

"I should've known. They haven't exactly been enthusiastic about the change, have they?"

"No," Jessica said with a sigh. "But maybe they'll learn to like it."

Mary Jo chuckled. "Maybe…if the single women keep coming."

"I think I'll go out and greet our guests, see if they have any complaints."

"All right. I think we're ready for the hors d'oeuvres soon."

"Thanks, Mary Jo."

When she entered the dining room, there were three or four groups already down. She was chatting with some of the guests when someone took her arm.

She jerked her head around to find Jim standing there. "What do you want?" she asked sharply.

"I wanted to invite you to join me at this other table. Some of the guests want to meet you."

Unable to refuse because the guests had requested it, she pulled her arm free and said, "Certainly. I'd be glad to."

He led her to the back table where two couples were seated and pulled out a chair for her. "Here, Jess. Sit down. They wanted to ask you some questions."

She smiled at the guests. "What did you want to ask me?"

One of the women spoke up. "How did you manage to keep your heart safe around all these good-looking cowboys?"

Jessica laughed, ignoring Jim. "Oh, we all have our crosses to bear, you know."

The door to the kitchen opened and several ladies brought out hors d'oeuvres trays.

"Well, it was nice meeting you. I'd better grab a seat while—"

She realized all the tables were full except that one. And Jim was standing by the only other seat—across from her.

He sat down. "Looks like we're stuck with each other tonight, Jess," he said, his lips spread in a smug smile.

"YOU DON'T NEED TO STAY, Jim. Leslie, Granddad and I can handle the bingo tonight."

They'd just gotten up from the table and she was hoping to be rid of him.

"That's all right. I like bingo. I see your brothers are going to play, too."

That was all she needed. "You'd better tell them they can't win. They can let their girlfriends win the prize if they choose, but they can't take it."

"Okay, I'll let them know."

She drew a deep breath as he walked away. Everyone had been asked to wait half an hour for the tables to be cleared before returning to that area for the game.

Determined to get started as soon as possible, Jessica began to help clearing up. When she was ready, she set up the bingo at one table and placed cards on the other tables, each with a bowl of uncooked pinto beans for markers. She rang the dinner bell to signal the guests back to the dining room.

Surprisingly, everyone returned. Even Jim.

Jim sat at the first table next to a little boy. It seemed he'd told the parents he'd help the boy so they could enjoy playing. He explained the rules to the boy, then Jessica saw him switch his card and have the boy call out bingo. The child was so excited he could hardly manage to get the numbers out. When Leslie confirmed that he'd won, he walked to the table with Jim to pick out a prize. The smile on his face made the shopping worthwhile.

As they walked back to their seats, she couldn't help turning her own smile on Jim. The gesture was thoughtful; the man himself showed his sweet side.

When the evening was over, Jessica figured the men would escort the guests to their cabins, leaving her to gather up the cards and the beans. However, she was wrong. Jim had Cliff, Pete and Hank escort the guests. He stayed to help her.

"Why aren't you escorting the guests?"

"Your brothers and Cliff are doing that. I'm helping you."

"I don't need any help."

"Yes, you do."

"Fine. Pick up the cards."

"Sure," he agreed.

They were finished in no time.

"That was quick," Jim said.

"Yes, good night." She turned on her heel to leave the room.

He reached out to stop her. "Wait a minute. We're

going to have another meeting when they get back. Come to the kitchen with me. I'll put on the coffee."

She shrugged off his hand. "I don't see a need for a meeting."

He raised his eyebrows. "If we have a meeting on a regular basis, we'll avoid any emergencies."

She didn't argue with him.

"You want to put out the coffee mugs?" he asked, as if they were best friends getting together for a visit.

She said nothing, setting them beside the coffeepot. Though his gaze rested on her, she ignored him and took the chair at the far end of the table. Determined not to talk to him, she clasped her hands and stared at the wall.

"Are you going to ignore me?"

"Of course not," she said, staring at her hands.

"I thought things went well tonight."

"Yes."

"I want you to go on the overnight camping trip this week. It's scheduled for Thursday night. Are you okay with that?"

"Who's going?"

"Hank and you…and me."

"No, I don't want to go."

"Why?"

She shrugged her shoulders.

"I'll require more of an answer than that, Jess," he said, just as the other three came into the kitchen.

Cliff frowned. "What's wrong?"

"I was telling Jessica I wanted her to go on the overnight camping trip, since we have some women going on it."

"Good thinking. Jessie loves camping out, anyway."

"I'm glad." Jim smiled smugly, as if the situation was settled.

"Is anyone listening?" Jessica blurted, her voice high, loud. "I don't want to go!"

Cliff stared at his granddaughter. "What's wrong with you, Jessie? You always like camping out."

"I don't see a need for me to go. I have a lot going on here."

"But, Jessie, what if one of the women gets hurt? Or sick? She's not going to want to deal with Hank or Jim."

"I don't think both Jim and I should be gone at the same time. There could be problems here."

"Leslie is going to stay in your room Thursday night so there will be a woman here. It'll work out great." Cliff nearly beamed at his granddaughter.

She didn't have the heart to argue with him. He was so pleased with Leslie working at the ranch. Her grandmother had died more than ten years ago. She didn't know how Leslie felt about Cliff, but she knew he had hopes of not being alone anymore.

"Fine. I'll go," she said. "Is there anything else? If not, I'm going to bed."

"Don't you want some coffee?" Jim asked.

"No, thanks." She stood and left the room.

"What's gotten into the girl?" Cliff asked.

Jim shrugged his shoulders. "I couldn't say."

Chapter Seven

Thursday morning, Jim didn't attempt to sit with Jessica for fear at the last minute she'd withdraw from their overnight camping trip.

The staff and eight guests—six men and two women—were to leave at eight-thirty, so Hank had left to make sure all the horses were saddled on time.

After breakfast Jim went out to the barn, where he checked with Hank which horse was his. Hank introduced him to Biscuit.

"Interesting name," he said with a grin.

"It's because of his color, that's all. He's a good ride." Hank looked around. "Where's Jessie? Do you think she'll come?"

"I hope so."

"Yeah, she's a good cook at a campfire."

"Well, I hope Jess comes on the ride. I'd like to see her cooking out in the open air."

"You'll do more than see her cook. You'll have to help her. I'll be taking care of the horses. Did you bring a coat?"

"Yeah. And I'll be more than happy to help."

Suddenly, he heard her laughter. He looked over his shoulder and saw Jessica strolling to the barn with one of the couples going on the ride.

He led Buck to meet her, sure she was riding that horse.

She took the reins from him. "Thanks."

Pulling her horse so that he stood between them, she tied her saddlebags behind the saddle. She also tied a slicker in place.

"You've brought a slicker?" Jim asked.

"Rain is predicted this afternoon. Up in the mountains it comes down faster and harder."

"Do all our guests have slickers?"

"Yes, and Hank has one for you, too."

He was grateful. She could have left him unprepared. Turning back to Hank, he got his slicker and tied it in place.

"Are we taking tents?" he asked Hank.

"Yeah, two to a tent, except for ours. It's a little larger than the others so we'll have three."

Jim frowned. "Does Jess know?"

"Yeah. Do you think that's why she didn't want to go?"

"Possibly."

"Should I tell her it will be all right?"

"Nope. Just let her be."

Jim swung into the saddle and followed Hank out of the barn, leaving room for those still to mount. When everyone was ready, Hank said, "We're going to start out on level land. We'll go at a lope over that part, then we'll start climbing, and we'll keep it to a walk. Most of the trail is wide enough to ride two across. Occasionally, it will narrow to only one at a time. Okay?"

Everyone agreed.

Hank led the way and the coupled riders followed him. Jim hadn't realized he'd get to ride with Jessica. Maintaining a nonchalant attitude, he watched her out of the corner of his eye.

She rode stiffly beside him until the motion of the horses finally relaxed her. With her hat pulled down low over her face, she didn't look his way even once. So he enjoyed himself, keeping an eye on her.

They rode for several hours with only a few short breaks. Hank kept staring at the clouds gathering around the mountaintops. As they began to climb, he urged them to keep up. "We want to find some shelter if it starts raining."

He kept them moving in a trot, a more difficult pace for inexperienced riders.

Jessica glanced at Jim, obviously to see how he was handling the pace. He had no difficulty with that gait. Neither did she, of course. Smiling at her, he turned his gaze forward, but he continued to check her out with his lids lowered.

Riding beside her was a pleasure he hadn't expected. He was so entranced that he wasn't paying attention to the weather.

Suddenly Jessica pulled to a halt.

Jim did likewise. "What's wrong, Jess?"

Without saying anything, she gestured to the sky. She began untying her slicker. He immediately did so, too. Hank had warned the others just before the rain started.

Pulling on his slicker, Jim asked, "Is there any shelter close by?"

Jessica shook her head. "We've got a couple of hours before we reach some shelter. That's where we're having lunch."

The rain quickly picked up. They were facing into it so their hats didn't do them much good. The wind picked up, too, and Jessica grabbed her hat just as the wind was lifting it off her head.

"Are you okay?" he yelled.

"Fine!" she called back.

Hank encouraged his riders to keep up, but they couldn't go any faster than a trot. When they turned away from the rain, the riding became a little easier for a while. But then the horses began to slip in the mud and Hank was forced to slow to a walk.

"We'll find some shelter just a little farther along. Just keep riding," Hank urged.

After another half hour, they turned another corner and there were some rock formations that they rode under. Hank got down and the other riders did, too. Jim and Jessica were the last to ride under the shelter. Hank gathered the reins of the other horses and led them to the edge, keeping them out of the rain. Jim joined him and held some of the reins.

Jessica told everyone to take out his or her bagged lunch. They would eat here. Then she took the reins Hank was holding. "Go eat your lunch, Hank. When you finish, I'll eat."

"Sis, you've got to keep the reins firm. Lightning will scare them."

"I know. Go eat."

She and Jim stood there holding twelve reins. When the lightning started, followed by thunder, Jim looked at Jessica. "Can you hold on?"

"Yes!" she answered, shouting over the thunder.

"Good thing your brother knew of this rock shelter."

"Yes. We'd hoped the rain wouldn't catch us. Hopefully it'll end soon."

"Yeah, because it will be hard to build a fire tonight."

"We carry some dry wood, just in case."

After a little while, Hank came back along with one of the men to hold the horses while she and Jim ate. They both got their lunches out of their saddle-bags. The others were standing around, but Jessica sat down on the dusty floor. Jim joined her.

"What did Mary Jo pack for us?" he asked.

"Ham and cheese sandwiches, a pickle and a banana-nut muffin."

"Sounds good."

Even better was sharing his lunch with Jessica. She didn't seem as mad at him as she'd been before. And he'd missed her. It sounded crazy to admit that, but he'd been enjoying hanging out with her over the past few days. Until he'd upset her.

"How much farther do we have to ride?" he asked.

"Another four hours, which wouldn't be bad, except for the rain. It'll be miserable if we have to make camp in this."

"I guess so. But you think you can cook in the rain?"

"Yes. I've done it before, as long as we have dry wood."

"Okay. You'll have to tell me what to do. Hank said I would be your helper because he'll be busy with the horses."

"Are you any good at cooking?"

He grinned. "I wouldn't starve to death, but I wouldn't win any prizes, either."

They ate their meal in peace. It was nice not to have her angry with him. In spite of the cold, damp air and uncomfortable rock beneath them, he was content.

When Hank signaled it was time to move on, he gave a pep talk to the guests. They showed little enthusiasm, but they remounted, their slickers in place, and rode out into the wind and rain.

About halfway into the ride, the rain changed to snow.

Jessica whispered to Jim. "Look!"

He snapped his head up, expecting to find an animal or something noteworthy. He hadn't expected snow. "This is better than rain, isn't it?"

"Yes, but the temperature has dropped quite a bit. The guests will have a trip to remember, that's for sure."

When they reached the area where they were going to camp, Jim noticed the fire pit, rimmed in rocks, obviously used many times. He also noticed the cleared ground, ensuring a reasonably comfortable sleep.

While Hank dealt with the horses, he lent a hand setting up the tents in a circle around the campfire. The snow hadn't let up, but it wasn't sticking to the ground much yet. As soon as he had all the tents up, including the larger tent for the three of them, he moved to the fire.

Jessica already had the fire going. Several of the guests were holding out their hands to the warmth.

"What do I do first?" he asked her.

"Peel potatoes. Then slice them as thin as possible."

She had set a pot of beans on a rock near the fire. Then she dragged some hot coals from the fire and set up a grill over the coals. She laid out eleven steaks, seasoning them with a little salt and pepper.

Then she mixed up biscuit dough and put it in a Dutch oven. By then, Jim had the potatoes ready. She heated up some grease in a big skillet and dumped the potatoes in to fry. Some of the guests had gone into their tents to store away their belongings, while others were gathered around the fire watching Jessica and Jim cook.

The best moment since they'd left home was when Jessica called everyone to eat. They used tin plates and grabbed their food and started eating at once. There were strategically placed boulders for them to use as seats. Several of them squatted on their haunches, cowboy-style.

"Man, this is good food!" one of the men said.

Others agreed. Jessica said thank you, but she didn't make a big deal of it. Jim thought they should give her a standing ovation, turning out this kind of meal in freezing conditions.

He left part of a big rock for her and was pleased when she accepted his offer. They were close enough to feel the heat from the fire.

"Did you get all the horses taken care of?" Jim asked as Hank sat down near them.

"Yeah. We built a small corral up here awhile ago so the horses wouldn't have to be tied up."

"Oh, I hadn't noticed it. Where is it?"

"Just around the corner, behind the rocks," Hank said.

"We thought this place would lend itself to an enjoyable trip," Jessica said, "but we didn't plan on rain or snow."

"I think you coped with it really well."

"Thanks. We'd planned on Hank playing his harmonica and all of us singing, but I'm sure everyone will want to turn in early."

Jim knew he wanted to. Sharing a tent with Jessica would be great. Especially if she slept beside him.

WHAT LIGHT THERE HAD BEEN in the Colorado sky had disappeared as everyone finished dinner. Jessica began collecting the empty plates; Jim gathered the cooking utensils. He figured he'd help Jessica wash them in a mountain stream Hank had mentioned wasn't too far away.

He reached for a flashlight, too.

"Ready?"

She whirled around. "Oh! Yes, I guess so."

"You'd better carry the flashlight," he said, "so you can lead the way."

"All right."

The stream was much closer than he'd thought. They knelt down and rinsed the dinnerware.

"I appreciate your help, Jim. It was nice of you to volunteer."

"You shouldn't have to do the cleanup at all, Jess. You cooked a damn fine meal."

"Thank you."

"Do you think anyone is going to want a sing-along now?"

"I wouldn't, if I were them. But some guests will expect it. We should definitely go ahead with it."

"Okay." He could wait a little while before he settled down next to her. But would he get any sleep?

They returned to the campfire to discover Hank playing the harmonica.

"He's good!" Jim whispered.

"I know." She sat down on a rock, leaving room for Jim. He immediately joined her. When Hank finished that song, she said, "How about we sing along? Play something we know, Hank."

He played several songs and Jessica led the singing. She had a great voice and invited the others to participate.

After half an hour, there was a general exodus.

Jessica and Jim watched as the others entered their tents. Before they realized it, Hank had gone into their tent.

"I need to excuse myself," Jessica said. Jim handed over the flashlight and sat by the fire while she was gone. When she came back, she handed the flashlight to him. He prepared for bed and approached their tent. The fire had been banked up, though it still gave out heat.

He pulled back the flap on the tent and looked at the arrangement. As he'd hoped, Jessica was in the middle. He crawled into the sleeping bag on the right side.

As soon as he settled down, he took a deep breath of Jessica's scent. She had a warm earthy smell mixed with a light scent that she always wore. After a minute he whispered, "Jess?"

"Yes?" she whispered back.

"Are you warm enough?"

"Yes."

"Okay. I just wanted to check."

"Go to sleep, Jim."

"Yeah," he agreed. What else could he do?

Lying there, he imagined her pressed against him, seeking his warmth as he sought hers. His fantasies led him to relax and before he knew it, he was asleep. With an arm over Jessica.

THE NEXT MORNING, JESSICA was awakened by her brother getting up. She was so warm and content, she

didn't want to get up. Instead she snuggled up to—
She jerked awake, aware of an arm holding her.

Shoving the arm away, she rudely awakened Jim.
"What were you doing with your arm on me?" she
demanded.

Jim sat up, blinking his eyes.

When he didn't answer at once, she asked him
again. "What was your arm doing across me?"

"I—I was just trying to get warm," he said, wishing
he could come up with a better reason, she guessed.

"Get up. We've got to get breakfast started." Her
voice was steely.

She stepped out of the tent, pulling on her coat.
Damn it. She'd been lulled into accepting him again
and he'd snuggled up to her during the night. When
would she learn? The most important duty right
now was getting the fire going. She wasn't going
to wait for Jim to do the work. He didn't seem to
be moving too fast.

When he stepped out of the tent, she said, "Did
you gather your belongings? Hank is going to pack
the tent up in a minute."

"No, I—I'll get them out."

Coming out of the tent a moment later, he brought
his coat, which he should've been wearing, and his
saddlebags.

"What can I do to help?"

"Watch the meat cooking while I mix up the
biscuits."

She didn't wait to see if he followed her order.

Mixing the biscuit dough didn't take long and she had the biscuits on the fire in no time. He'd taken out the sausages. She wiped out the skillet and put in all the eggs, scrambling them with a fork.

"Should I wake up all the guests?"

"Yes, please."

He called to each tent.

Jessica took up the biscuits and set them next to the sausages. Then she pulled the skillet off the fire so the eggs wouldn't burn.

"Please bring all your belongings out of the tent and roll your bedrolls," she advised the guests. "Hank will begin taking down the tents immediately."

They returned to their tents to do as she said.

"Breakfast is served!" she called.

The guests made their way to the fire to take a plate with sausages, scrambled eggs and biscuits.

Jessica finished filling their plates and discovered Jim standing beside her. "Here's your plate."

"Where's Hank?"

"He's saddling the horses."

"I'll go see if I can help him."

She nodded and ate the food she'd fixed for him.

Both men returned to the fire a couple of minutes later and she divided what was left for them. When Jim sat down, she gathered up the other plates and mugs and took them to the stream. Jim showed up a couple of minutes later as she was finishing. Leaving him to take care of his and Hank's dishes, she returned to the fire to pack up.

She felt his presence beside her before she heard
him ask, "Are you going to talk to me ever again?"
Jessica didn't answer him.

Chapter Eight

For the rest of the morning she talked to the two women on the trip, partnering up with one of them. The woman's husband came to Jim.

"Looks like we're riding together," Bob said with a smile.

"Sure thing," Jim agreed. As he settled into the procession, he looked at Jessica.

He hadn't intended to do anything to upset her. Putting his arm around her last night had been a reflex, he assured himself. If he'd stayed awake all night, he wouldn't have done such a stupid thing. The worst part was that he felt he'd gained some closeness with her that had been wiped away when she'd found his arm around her.

"Did you upset Jessica?" Bob asked.

"Why would you ask that?"

"Hell, I'm just looking for a fellow sufferer. I had the wrong idea last night. I wanted to make love and my wife absolutely refused."

"It was a little public last night. The tents weren't far apart."

"Yeah, but I'm her husband!"

Jim only raised his brows, keeping his opinion to himself.

"I know. I shouldn't have tried. She doesn't do well in less-than-cushy circumstances."

"I gather the overnight trail ride was your decision?"

"Yeah, she wasn't so much for it. She wanted to go shopping again in Steamboat Springs."

"Why didn't you let her go to Steamboat and come on the trail ride on your own?"

"Because men are drawn to her. I can't leave her alone!" the man growled.

Jim looked at Bob's wife. She was attractive, to be sure, but Jim was definitely drawn to Jessica, not the other woman. Jessica was fresh-faced this morning, not needing makeup to look beautiful.

Bob's wife looked irritated and uncomfortable. Still it was unfair for him to judge her, since Jess had been born to this life and she hadn't. But she might have tried a smile—a smile would've gone a long way to convince any man.

When they broke for lunch, Jessica made sandwiches for everyone. Jim decided she must be tired of preparing all the food. She'd probably be glad to get back to the ranch.

When she handed him his lunch, he thanked her and didn't complain about not riding with her, though he wanted to. Instead, he had to listen to the man next to him. He didn't think that marriage would last long.

Coming down the mountain, they were afforded great views of the valley and the surrounding mountains. As they reached level ground, Jim's partner left him to ride beside his wife. Hank increased the pace to a lope once again, and Jim moved up to ride beside Jessica.

She didn't look at him or stay up with him. He held his horse back until she shot him an angry look.

"Look, Jess, it was an accident. I didn't mean anything by it. I didn't even know what you were concerned about until I was fully awake. You can't hold that against me."

"Maybe not, but I don't think I want to share a tent with you again."

At least she was talking to him again. "But it wasn't my fault."

"Then whose fault would it be?"

He shrugged his shoulders. "I guess it was an accident."

She let out a big sigh. "Okay, I'll admit I may have overreacted."

And that was one of the things that made her so...so attractive. "That's big of you, Jess. I promise I didn't mean to...to take advantage of you."

"Let's just forget it."

He was all for that.

They rode in silence for a few minutes until he spoke. "Did Bob's wife complain about him?"

She turned to look at him. "What do you mean?"

"He told me what happened."

"I don't know what you're talking about."

"He wanted to—to make love and she rejected him."

"In a tent? Is he crazy?"

"Maybe."

"No, she didn't mention that, and I can see why."

"Yeah, me, too."

Jessica shook her head. "Sometimes I think we're like psychologists. The guests share more than we want to know."

"That's true. It's happened to you?"

"Yes, particularly with women who want certain men to notice them."

"Hey, you're not talking about me! I haven't been here that long. Must be your brothers."

She rolled her eyes and said nothing.

"Me? What woman is after me?"

"Miranda, the woman we gave private lessons to. She wanted you to notice her more than anything. She complained about it during the lesson."

"That's nonsense! I didn't give her any reason to think—"

"I know you didn't. I was there."

"Did you tell her that?"

"Of course not! I want her to come back and chase you again!" She grinned at him.

"Low blow, Jess."

"Turnabout, Jim."

He chuckled. Maybe she had a point there. He wasn't sure.

All he knew was that the animosity had disappeared and he enjoyed the rest of the ride.

When they turned to the barn, Leslie was waiting for them.

"How are things here?" Hank asked as he swung down from his horse.

Leslie seemed to gulp. "Cliff took Pete to the hospital in Steamboat Springs. He had an accident."

Hank dropped his reins. "What kind of accident?"

"It was silly. He tripped over one of the guests and—"

"How badly is he hurt?" Jessica asked.

"He broke a leg."

"Is everything else all right?" Jim asked, "or are there other things we need to deal with?"

Leslie shook her head. "I offered some lessons in bridge playing, and I got Mitch to give roping lessons again to the boys and their fathers." She reached out to hug Jessica. "Oh, I'm so glad all of you are back!"

Jessica left her horse to Jim and walked back in with Leslie. "I'm sorry you had to deal with so much, but I can't thank you enough."

"I didn't mind, Jessica. I was just worried about Pete and Cliff. When Cliff called a few minutes ago, he sounded so depressed."

"It's understandable. I suspect Hank will want to go to the hospital. If he doesn't, I will."

The phone was ringing as they approached

Leslie's desk. She rushed forward and lifted the receiver. "Lazy L Ranch," she said. Then, "Oh, Cliff, I'm so glad you called. Jessica's here." She handed her the phone.

"Granddad, how is Pete?"

"He's having a hard time, but they're putting on his cast now."

"So there wasn't much swelling?"

"No. It was a clean break and will just take six weeks to heal if he's reasonably careful."

"When has he ever been reasonable?" she asked.

"I know, but maybe he'll stop to think this time. We'll be home in half an hour. No need for you or Hank to come."

"Okay. We'll be waiting for you."

She repeated her grandfather's words to Leslie. "I'd better go out and tell Hank."

Back in the barn, she found Hank and Jim hurriedly unsaddling the horses. She told them the latest news.

Hearing he'd be laid up for six weeks, Hank groaned. "Man, what are we going to do?"

"Make do. We'll see who Pete thinks should handle the cattle while he's laid up. We'll manage."

"That's right, Hank," Jim said. "We can all pull together. I can take over the horses if you want to take care of the cattle. With Jess's help, we can give lessons and lead an overnight trail ride if we need to."

"I guess. Damn him for breaking his leg!"

"Don't be so hard on him, Hank," Jessica said. "I'm sure he didn't plan on it." She patted her brother's shoulder. "Now, I'd better go check with Mary Jo and make sure she hasn't had any disasters."

"Wait a second and I'll go with you, Jess," Jim said. "We're finishing up here."

She wasn't sure why she should wait for him, but Jim was too hard to turn down.

A minute later, he'd put away the last of the tack and reached Jessica's side to take her hand.

"What are you doing?" she asked, drawing her hand out of his.

"Just being friendly."

"I think you'd better rethink that, Jim. You were just being friendly last night, too, right?"

"That was an accident."

"Maybe. But I don't think holding hands would be considered an accident."

He raised one brow. "Maybe not, but it could be considered friendly."

Jessica couldn't hold back a smile.

When they reached the kitchen, Mary Jo greeted them. "You're back! How did it go?"

Jessica sighed. "Better than here, I'm told."

"So you've heard about Pete." She hung her head. "He tripped because he wasn't paying attention. He was arguing with me."

Jessica stared at her friend. "What about?"

"He thought I shouldn't come out of the kitchen."

Jessica's eyebrows knitted in confusion. "What?"

"I went out to see if anyone wanted any extra dessert, but Pete didn't think that was appropriate."

"I don't know what to say," Jessica said.

Jim spoke up. "I do, Mary Jo. Don't worry about anything. It's ridiculous to think offering any more food would be wrong. I'll talk to him."

Mary Jo lowered her gaze. "I wasn't trying to get him in trouble, Jim, really. I just didn't know if I was doing something wrong."

"You weren't," Jessica assured her friend. "By the way, they're on their way home. Would you mind fixing him a tray? I'll take it into him once he's settled."

"Sure, I'll do that."

Jim followed Jessica out of the kitchen. "I bet Pete's mood is rotten right now."

"Yes, I would guess so."

"What's planned for this evening?"

"Another movie. Billy Crystal in *City Slickers*."

"They're not going to want to take a calf home with them, are they?" Jim asked with a grin.

"No, I don't think so. But it will give the people who went on the overnight ride a chance to go to bed without missing anything important."

"True. How about us?"

"Granddad and I can handle tonight if you want to go to bed early."

"When will you start it?"

"At seven."

"I should be able to stay up that late."

"Your choice."

"What about Pete? Will he feel like watching?"

"Granddad said it was a clean break and they got

him to the doctor before there was much swelling, so I expect he's feeling all right. If we put him in a chair and prop up his leg, he might watch."

As if on cue Leslie called out to her. "They're here."

Jessica hurried to the front door, waiting there for her brother and grandfather. Jim slipped past her. "I'd better see if I can help."

"Thanks, Jim."

She watched her brother negotiate the walk by leaning on Jim and Cliff. She was waiting by the door when he reached it. "How are you, Pete?"

"I'm damn fine!" he snapped.

"Now, boy, don't take your anger out on your sister," Cliff counseled.

"Mary Jo has fixed you a supper tray. Why don't you go to bed?" Jessica suggested.

"I don't want her food!"

Jessica was taken aback. "Pete, I don't understand what's wrong."

"It's her fault I'm hurt! I told her not to serve anyone, but she insisted."

"Why did that matter? What would a late dessert hurt anything?"

"I told her not to! That's what matters!"

"You mean you ordered her not to serve food and she did anyway? That's the problem?"

"Yeah!"

Jessica threw out her hands. "Pete, you're being ridiculous!"

Jim stepped forward, putting his hand on her arm,

as if to stop her tirade. "Let's get him to bed, Jess. We'll deal with whatever is going on here once we get him settled." He moved Pete toward the kitchen.

Pete resisted. "I don't want to go in there!"

"It's the only way to get to the back bedrooms, unless you want to walk all the way around the house to the back door."

"Pete, I'll ask Mary Jo to look away while you come through the kitchen. Okay?" Jessica asked.

"All right, as long as she turns her back!"

Jessica went through the kitchen door. "Mary Jo, will you turn your back so we can bring Pete in through here? I'd appreciate it."

"Of course," Mary Jo said.

"He's coming through now."

As she promised, Mary Jo turned her back as Jim brought Pete through the kitchen.

Jessica made a deal with the heavens. She'd give anything to know what really happened between Mary Jo and her brother.

AFTER PETE HAD EATEN his dinner, Jessica took his tray to the kitchen. When she put the tray on the counter, she pulled Mary Jo aside. "What happened between you and Pete?"

Mary Jo looked away, then she repeated her story.

Jessica shook her head. "It doesn't make sense. Something more than that happened."

"Do you want me to resign?"

"What? No! That makes even less sense!"

"Look, we had an argument. He was mad at me and I was determined not to give in to him. We'd been— I didn't— I shouldn't have had anything to do with him, but your brother is a very persuasive man. A very handsome man." Tears filled her eyes. "It might be better if I leave."

"I don't understand. Do you mean you were dating?"

"Not exactly. But—but I slept with him. I realized I'd made a mistake so I told him I wasn't going to sleep with him again."

"Oh, mercy! Mary Jo, I had no idea!"

The tears began to fall now. "I'm so sorry, Jessica. I tried to resist him, but then I thought, why not? But it turns out he was just using me."

Jessica hugged her. "It's all right, Mary Jo. You're not leaving and he's not going to bother you again."

"If you change your mind, just tell me. I don't want you to get into trouble with your family."

"No, Mary Jo. That won't happen."

After reassuring her again, she left the kitchen and headed for Leslie's desk. She knew she would find her grandfather there.

"We need to have a meeting," she told him without preamble. "Where's Jim?"

"I think he went to get cleaned up before dinner. But we can handle it. What's wrong?"

She shook her head. "You put him in charge, Granddad. I think we need him."

"Well, can't it wait until dinner? I'm hungry."

"You'll be a lot hungrier if Mary Jo leaves!" Jessica shot back at him. She couldn't believe he was being difficult.

"What are you talking about?" Leslie asked.

"Mary Jo offered to resign."

Both Cliff and Leslie stared at her in shock.

"Well, she must have a secret!" Cliff decided.

"Yes, she does."

"But, Jessie, what is it?"

"I don't want to tell you just yet."

Jim came through the kitchen then, apparently looking for Jessica. "Here you are."

"Yes, I've been waiting for you," Jessica said.

"I like to hear that," he assured her, shooting her a smile.

"You won't when you find out why."

Chapter Nine

Jim's smile morphed into a serious look. "What's wrong?"

She shot a look at her grandfather. "I'd rather tell you in private."

"Hey, you can't do that, little girl," Cliff protested. "You've already told us there's a problem. I demand to know what it is."

With her eyes she pleaded for Jim to insist on privacy.

"I think maybe I'd better talk to Jess alone. But I'll tell you the problem later, I promise. Right, Jess?"

"Yes."

"All right. Come on, Jess." This time when he took her hand, she didn't protest.

He led her back to his bedroom, the only place he could be assured of privacy. When he shut the door he turned to her. "Now, what is the problem?"

"Pete talked Mary Jo into sleeping with him." She swallowed. "Then when she decided she'd made a mistake—I don't know why—she said she didn't want to sleep with him anymore. That's why they were having an argument. Pete was being difficult and decided to order Mary Jo to stay in the kitchen. She was determined to do her job and came out offering extra desserts. He came after her and that's when he tripped."

Jim ran a hand through his hair. "That's quite a story." He took a moment to digest it—and the potential legal ramifications—then said, "Would you mind asking Mary Jo to step in here if she can spare the time? It's best if we talk to her right away."

He sat there waiting for Jess to return. He suspected that Mary Jo realized too late that Pete was using her, but he'd wait to hear her story.

His door opened and Jess returned with Mary Jo in tow.

"Hi, Mary Jo. Jess told me the problem you and Pete are having. We wondered if you could tell us why you're upset with Pete. It will make it easier for me when I talk to him if I know."

Mary Jo sent a stricken look to Jessica.

"It's okay, Mary Jo. He won't hold it against you."

Mary Jo flopped on the bed, the only place to sit. "I—I was attracted to Pete and he seemed to be to me. The evening was wonderful. But then he hooked up with one of the guests and slept with her! When I found out, I was horrified and I told him we were through."

Jessica rubbed her friend's shoulder. "I'm so sorry, Mary Jo."

"You two wait here." Jim turned to the door. "I'm going to go talk to Pete."

Mary Jo jumped up. "I can't wait. I have to go finish up dinner." Mary Jo looked at Jessica, not Jim.

"You go ahead. I'll talk to you later," Jessica said.

After Mary Jo left, she turned to Jim. "I'm going with you."

"I think it would be better if I spoke to him alone."

"No!"

Jim sighed. "Prepare yourself for what may be a difficult conversation."

"I've been in a few difficult conversations."

He led the way next door to Pete's room. At Jim's knock, Pete yelled, "Come in."

"Hello, Pete. Mind if we come in for a little talk?" Jim asked.

"No, come on in."

Pete looked surprised to see his sister follow Jim in. The room had one chair in it, and Jessica took it, leaving the edge of the bed for Jim.

He settled himself and asked, "Can you explain what was going on when you broke your leg?"

He looked really annoyed. "I've already told the story. I ordered Mary Jo to stay in the kitchen, and she defied me!" Anger rose in his voice.

"Why would you do that?"

"Why not? I'm the boss."

"Maybe I should tell you Jessie has been talking to Mary Jo."

Pete clamped his mouth shut and glared at his sister.

Jim spoke before he could curse her.

"We know you had sex with Mary Jo. We know you then had sex with one of the guests. Mary Jo didn't want to be with you again, and so she refused you."

"So? That doesn't mean she should defy me!"

Jessica's anger got the best of her. "How could you be so asinine?"

Jim interrupted. "We don't need to trade insults. Pete, Mary Jo could sue us for sexual harassment, and she'd win. Fortunately, I don't think she's going to do that, as long as you have nothing to do with her again. No flirting, no pressure, no nothing. Do you understand?"

"Hey, we didn't make any promises!" Pete protested.

"When you are intimate with someone, you've made a promise, even though the words weren't spoken. Unless you tell her it was just for fun, and she understands *before* you have sex, you've made a promise."

"I didn't—"

"You don't have a choice, Pete."

"But—"

"And you'd better make sure the guest you had relations with understands that, also. If not, she may sue us, too. And from now on, stay away from the female guests. Do you understand?"

"Yeah, fine!"

"Good. We'll hold you to that promise."

He stood and Jessica joined him. She didn't look at her brother.

After they left the room, she said to Jim, "Do you believe what you said?"

"About what?"

"That if you have sex with a woman, you've made a promise to sleep only with her? Even if you don't put it into words?"

"Yes, I believe that. Why?"

"Never mind. I was just wondering." Then she asked, "Are you going to inform Granddad?"

"Yeah, I'll take care of it."

"Go ahead and eat. I'll talk to Mary Jo first."

"Okay. Tell her to let me know if Pete puts any pressure on her, no matter how slight."

"I will." She smiled at him.

He walked away with that smile printed on his soul.

JESSICA WAITED IN THE kitchen until Mary Jo looked up and saw her.

"Have you finished preparing dinner?"

"Yes. You'd better get a seat so you can eat."

"I want to talk to you first."

Mary Jo took a deep breath. "Okay. I can talk now."

They both went to Jessica's bedroom.

"Do I have to quit?"

"Absolutely not!" Jessica said. "We talked to Pete. Jim told him he was in the wrong. He said Pete had made a promise to you of exclusivity unless you both agreed it was just for fun beforehand. He said you could sue for sexual harassment and win, if he didn't tell you it meant nothing."

"He didn't."

Jessica could hear the sadness in Mary Jo's voice. She knew the heartache Mary Jo was experiencing because she had suffered when her boyfriend was two-timing her.

"Jim made him promise no pressure, no flirting, no nothing."

"I see. And he agreed?"

Jessica said, "Yes."

"Okay. So—so Jim thinks I can stay?"

"Absolutely. Pete was wrong, ordering you to stay in the kitchen. There was no rhyme nor reason for such an order."

"I know," Mary Jo said softly.

Jessica heaved a sigh. "I know it will be hard, Mary Jo, but I don't want you to go."

"I don't want to, either, but…"

"Just try it for a while, okay?"

"Okay."

"I'm going to go get my supper. Thanks, Mary Jo."

"Sure. If there isn't any left, come back to the kitchen and I'll find something for you."

Jessica opened the door to the dining room and saw that Jim had saved her a seat and some food.

"Thanks," she said softly as she sat beside him.

"Everything okay?" he asked.

"Yes, so far." She picked up her fork and started eating. Jim fielded all the questions their dinner mates asked while she ate.

Dessert was served as she finished her meat loaf. Tonight it was carrot cake, one of her favorites.

"This is really good," one of the female guests exclaimed.

"Yes, it's one of the specialties of our chef," Jessica bragged.

"I've really started looking forward to the desserts. I don't think anything she cooks is bad, but her desserts are over the top. I'm afraid I'm gaining weight!" the woman complained.

"You get to go home after a week. I have to deal with those desserts every day!" Jessica complained with a laugh.

"I don't see a problem," Jim assured her. "You look beautiful to me."

She blushed and accepted the compliment with a nod and a smile. "It's hard, though."

He looked just as beautiful to her.

THEY WERE SHOWING *City Slickers* tonight. Due to the popularity of the film, they had a full house. Jim saved Jessica a seat near the back of the room. After introducing the film, she slipped into the chair next to him and he immediately took her hand and held it on his thigh. She felt tremors run through her body and hoped he didn't feel the vibrations.

In the dim light, he smiled at her, and she knew he was aware what he did to her. But his talk with Pete had loosened something in her resistance. Jim wouldn't betray a woman he was sleeping with.

Unlike the last time she'd shared her body. It gave her pause for thought.

Partway through the film, Jim dropped her hand and wrapped his arm around her. She froze. He'd never been that close to her. But after a minute, she relaxed against him, finding it a comfortable fit.

Just before the film ended, he dipped his head and briefly touched her lips with his. She loved·the feel of his mouth on hers, however brief. And she found herself wanting more. But the lights were turned on.

He pulled her up and said, "I'll help escort the guests to the cabins. Then I'll be back."

"Are we having a meeting?"

"Not tonight. But wait up for me."

She didn't want to speculate why she should wait up for him. Maybe he needed to talk to her. Or maybe he hadn't talked to Cliff yet, and wanted her to support him. She didn't know why, but she'd do as he asked.

Secretly she hoped he just wanted another kiss.

Chills rushed through her at that thought as she waited in the kitchen.

It wasn't the first time she'd admitted that she was attracted to Jim. She'd fought it because she didn't want to be betrayed again. And she didn't think an affair with Jim would be appropriate.

She still didn't, but after what he said tonight, she knew if she gave in to temptation, he wouldn't break her heart. At least not without warning.

When the door opened, it was Jim alone who entered the kitchen.

"Did you talk to Granddad?"

"Yeah. He agreed with us that Pete was at fault."

"I'm glad."

"I noticed Mary Jo didn't bother to come to the movie. Have you seen her?"

"No. I figured she went to bed early."

He came closer. "Are you sleepy?"

"A little," she confessed.

"All right, then maybe you wouldn't mind a goodnight kiss."

Since he asked her, she felt she had to give him an answer. "I—I think I'd like that."

"Good, because I'm dying for it." He took her in his arms and kissed her, a kiss she felt in every part of her.

She slid her arms around his neck and encouraged him to touch her.

His arms ran up and down her back, and suddenly she knew she'd had enough—or not enough. Withdrawing, she whispered good-night and slipped out the door to her bedroom, anxious to reach it before he came after her.

Once her door was shut, she leaned against it, listening for his footsteps going to his room. She didn't hear anything.

She was torn. She didn't want to give in to any encouragement he offered, but she'd loved his kiss. Would she be able to withstand any invitation, verbal or physical, he made?

Did she even want to?

JIM TURNED AND LEFT THE kitchen. He was going outside—without his jacket. Some cool night air ought to relieve a problem he had.

When he stepped out the front door, drawing a deep breath, he interrupted another good-night kiss. Cliff was telling Leslie good-night in a familiar fashion.

He turned away, staring up at the stars. In New York, he seldom saw the stars. Out here, they were spectacular. He was looking up but his thoughts were on Jess. She was the brightest star he'd ever seen.

"You okay?" Cliff asked from behind him.

He spun around. "Yeah, sorry I interrupted you."

"No problem. We were…were just saying good-night."

"Leslie is a nice lady."

"Yes, she is. I'm going to ask her to marry me."

Jim shook his hand. "Good for you. I hope she says yes."

"Me, too. I've been alone for a while now. Everything I do will be made better by having Leslie to share with."

"I agree."

"You ever been married?"

"No. I was fairly serious about a woman in New York City. But I decided I didn't want to stay there. When I suggested that to her, she laughed at me and said I couldn't leave New York. I did and I told her we were through."

"How did she take it?"

"Not well. But I wasn't staying there. I didn't want to put down roots, build a family, when I was unhappy. That would've been a disaster."

"I agree. Well, I wish you well, Jim. Finding someone to share your life with is wonderful."

"Yeah."

Cliff turned toward the door. "I'm going to turn in." He looked back at Jim. "Aren't you cold?"

Jim sighed. "Yeah, I'm getting there."

"Why didn't you grab a coat?"

"It wasn't convenient. And I was a little overheated."

Not in the way you think, he silently added.

AFTER ALL THE FIREWORKS, the rest of the week was calm. The guests finished their week peacefully, unaware of all the problems. When they left, they were full of praise for their week's vacation.

The staff, meaning the family and Jim, sat down to a nice lunch. Pete, his leg propped up, kept his eye on the door to the kitchen. But Mary Jo had refused his invitation.

Jim was more relaxed today, happy with the way things were going. Jessica hadn't withdrawn from him at all. He'd gotten another good-night kiss last night. He'd wanted more, but he guessed she was still not sure of him. He'd have to be patient.

Sitting beside her, he leaned toward her and whispered, "I think he's looking for Mary Jo."

"I know. I'm glad she decided against joining us."

"I'm wondering what he's thinking."

She whispered back, "I have no idea."

"Is Leslie coming at one?" Cliff asked.

"Yes, she said she would help with the registration," Jessica told him. "Oh, and Hank, we'll need you to help with luggage today. Jim and Sam can't do it all on their own."

"Hey! I'm supposed to have Sunday off!"

"Your sister doesn't have it off. I don't see why you're special," Jim said quietly.

"But we agreed!"

"I think that was before I came. And I still don't see how it's fair for you and Pete to have the day off and not Jessica."

"Okay, but I don't like it."

"Hank, that's not very nice of you," Cliff said.

"Sorry, Granddad," Hank said with a hangdog air.

Jessica didn't say anything. She'd asked Hank's cooperation in front of Jim and her grandfather. She knew she could count on them. Unfair, maybe, but her brothers had forced her to do so by their attitudes.

Pete suddenly asked, "Do we get dessert for lunch?"

"No, I told Mary Jo we could do without dessert for lunch today. After all, she doesn't get a single day off. We're going to have to work that out soon. It's not fair to her."

"Well, Jessie, I guess you could fill in for her. After all, you don't have any set duties anymore." Pete glared at her.

Jim spoke up. "I don't think that's a good idea. She has a lot of duties."

"She did before you came," Pete snarled.

"Are you looking for a fight, Pete?" Jim asked calmly. "I don't mind fighting you, but it might be a little one-sided since you have a broken leg."

Pete was fuming.

"Boys, we'll have no fighting. Jim is right. We'll work something out for Mary Jo. She deserves a day off. But we don't have to decide it today." Cliff looked at all the males at the table.

"Sure," Jim said, not at all upset.

Leslie came in just then and Cliff jumped up to greet her.

Pete watched his grandfather. "The old fool's going to get trapped if he doesn't watch himself."

"Pete!" Jessica exclaimed.

"I think your grandfather will be lucky if Leslie accepts his proposal," Jim added. "But you'll have me to deal with if you say anything to your grandfather or Leslie."

"You think you're in control, don't you?" Pete asked.

"Yeah, I do."

Jessica interrupted the argument. "Pete, why don't you quit trying to ruin everyone else's party, just because you made a mistake."

"I didn't make a mistake."

"Then why are you so angry?"

"Just leave me alone. Hank, help me back to my room."

Hank got up to assist his brother. "I'll be back in a few minutes to help with the luggage."

Once her brothers were out of the room, she relaxed against the back of her chair. "What do you think was going on with Pete? He seems so bitter."

"I agree with you. I think he knows he made a mistake, but he doesn't want to admit it."

"Well, I hope he gets over it soon. I can't take this sparring much longer."

"Sure you can, honey. You know you're strong."

"I hope so. But we are going to have to make an adjustment to Mary Jo's schedule. I can take over one day a week, and—"

"I don't want you to."

"But it wouldn't be that difficult. I can cook."

"It's not that I doubt your abilities. I just don't want to lose you to the kitchen."

"I don't think one day would be that big a loss. If I cooked on Wednesday, then I think that would work out."

"If you insist. But let's wait until Pete is back on his feet."

"Maybe. I'll talk to Mary Jo about it."

Leslie poked her head in the dining room. "Jessica, the first arrivals are here."

"I'm coming," she called back.

Cliff had not driven to the airport today. They'd hired a bus service to meet their guests, who were expected a bit later. These guests had made their own way.

She and Jim went out to the reception area. There wasn't anything to identify the two men and two women who stood there.

Jessica was about to welcome them, when one of the women broke into a big smile and ran right to Jim.

"Jim! I'm so glad to see you!" And she planted a big kiss right on his lips.

Chapter Ten

Jessica's eyes widened at the woman's forward behavior. And even more at Jim, who seemed to kiss her back.

By the time he looked at Jessica, she turned to register the group. Inside, she was wondering who the woman was and what she meant to Jim. Did he have a relationship with her? Was he hoping to cheat on her with Jessica?

Outside, she was cordial and courteous. "May I have your names?" she requested calmly.

One of the men spoke for the group. "Sure, I'm Dub Jones, this is Melanie Cooper, Deke Bronkowski and the romantic one is Bronwyn Jefferson."

"Of course. I have your reservations. You'll be staying in cabin six. Here are your name tags. We ask that you wear them so we can identify you quickly and better serve you. I'll ask Jim to carry your luggage." She peeked over the counter at the pile of luggage the two men had carried in. "And Hank to accompany him. Dinner will be served at six. We hope you enjoy your stay."

"Yes, ma'am. I'm sure we will."

"Hank, would you help Jim carry the luggage to cabin six?"

"Sure," Hank agreed, giving a once-over to the woman who'd thrown herself at Jim. "Ready, Jim?"

"Yeah," Jim said, gently pushing the woman away from him. He turned to say something to Jessica, but she kept her back turned to him until she heard him lead the group to its cabin.

"That was interesting," Leslie said. "It says here they're from New York City."

"Yes, I remember. They were a last-minute reservation. I was so pleased because it meant we had a full house," Jessica said bitterly.

Leslie looked at her uncertainly. "You don't sound so happy about it now."

"No." Jessica didn't elaborate on her thinking. She didn't want to confess her feelings toward Jim. Especially not anymore.

Before she had time to dwell on the situation, the bus from the airport arrived with a large group of guests. Jessica and Leslie started processing the group as fast as they could. They had them leave their luggage in the lobby, promising to have their bags delivered shortly.

Jim and Hank came back in the front door and Jessica kept her gaze lowered.

"Jess, I need to talk to you," Jim said urgently.

"I'm sorry, but we promised you'd deliver the luggage. Please take those to room one." And then she turned away.

When Jim came down, he tried again to talk to her, but she sent him to cabin one.

He grabbed the bags and ran out the door.

Then she said to Leslie, "I'm going to run an errand. Would you ask the men to take the other bags to the cabins?"

"Sure, I'll be glad to."

"Thanks, Leslie."

She went out the back door and got into her car, which she kept parked in the back, and drove out the front driveway just as she saw Jim returning to the main building.

When she reached the end of the driveway, she headed for the right, because she was sure Jim was going to come after her and he would think she'd set out left toward Steamboat Springs.

She didn't want to see him.

JIM GOT LESLIE TO FREE HIM up and he chased out after Jessica. But by the time he reached the end of the driveway, she was out of sight.

He turned left and headed into town since Leslie had said Jess had an errand to run.

Once he got to town, he drove around trying to find Jessica's car. He went into the restaurant where they'd eaten. He asked after her in several shops. He walked the streets looking for her car. Finally he had to admit she'd vanished. At six o'clock he headed back to the ranch.

Lucky for him, Bronwyn hadn't tried to save him a seat in the dining room. Had she gotten the message that he wasn't interested in her? When he'd explained that to her earlier, she'd wanted to know who he *was* interested in.

He hadn't answered her.

Absentmindedly he took a seat with a family of five. The wife chatted on about the ranch and he listened with half an ear, unable to stop thinking about Jessica. Where had she gone?

The wife got his attention. "Where are you from?"

"Texas."

"We are, too! We're from Austin."

"I was from west Texas. But recently I've been working in New York City."

"Wow! That's different. What were you doing there?"

"Working on Wall Street."

"What brought you here?"

"I wanted to get back to country life. This job opened up and I took it."

The husband agreed. "Well, I think that's a good decision. I don't like city life, either."

Talking about city life made Jim think of Bronwyn again. Damn it, he thought. Things with Jessica were going so well until she came along.

He glanced at Bronwyn holding court over her table. What he used to see as confidence he now saw as conceit. She didn't even look as beautiful to him now. He much preferred a fresh-faced woman with natural beauty.

A woman like Jessica.

Where was she? Why had she disappeared?

There could be only one reason. She was upset about Bronwyn's kiss. That was good news, he rationalized, but not until he'd assured her he didn't love Bronwyn and hadn't known about her coming.

But would she believe him?

JESSICA SLIPPED IN THE BACK DOOR a little before ten. She'd spent the day driving around and finally stopped for dinner at a restaurant in a nearby small town.

Now she tiptoed down the hall and tapped lightly on Mary Jo's door. "It's Jessica. May I come in?"

Her friend opened the door immediately. "Where have you been? Everyone's been wondering where you took off to."

She sat down on the bed with a deep sigh. "I…couldn't stay here. Not after that scene in the lobby during registration."

Mary Jo looked lost. "What scene?"

Jessica remembered then that her friend had probably been in the kitchen, where she spent all her time. She was glad that they'd arranged for her to fill in as cook on Wednesdays.

She filled her in on the unfortunate details. "Our first guests arrived, and when one of the women saw

Jim, she broke into a smile and jumped into his arms, planting a kiss on him."

"No! That's terrible! What did he say?"

She lowered her gaze. "I didn't give him a chance to say anything. I scooted out before he got back from taking luggage to the cabins."

"You can't avoid him forever."

"No, but I can try." Tears welled in her eyes and her throat tightened. "He's been softening me up, making it sound like he'd never two-time anyone, but it looks like I was going to be his playmate until his real girl came along."

"Like Cal?"

Mary Jo was the only one who knew the whole story about her heartbreaking split with her college lover. And she was intuitive enough to realize how the incident with Jim brought back too many bad memories. "Yes. I won't do that again."

"I know. But Jim is not Cal. Maybe you should give him a chance."

The tears slid down Jessica's face now. "I can't."

JIM'S SPIRITS ROSE when he spotted Jessica's car out back. He knocked on her door.

No answer.

He knocked again, and then leaned his ear against the door.

Nothing.

He tried Mary Jo's door.

"Who is it?"

"It's Jim. Have you seen Jess?"

She came to the door, opening it a little, obviously dressed for bed. "Yes, I saw her. She came in a little while ago. She said she was tired and was going to sleep. If she didn't answer, I'd guess she's asleep already."

"How long ago?"

"About half an hour ago."

"How did she seem?"

"Fine. Why? Did something happen?"

"No! No, not at all. I was just surprised she didn't come back for dinner."

"She told me she went out. I don't blame her. Always eating the same cooking can get boring."

"So she wasn't meeting anyone?"

Mary Jo raised her brows. "I don't know. I didn't think to ask her that."

Jim frowned. "Okay. I'll let you get to sleep. Thanks for answering my questions."

"Sure. Good night, Jim."

He turned back to his room, disconsolate. He'd hoped to talk to Jessica this evening, to tell her how badly he'd handled the Bronwyn situation. But her arrival had shocked him, and her kiss had been unexpected. By the time he'd tried to speak to Jessica, she wouldn't even look at him. And she'd kept him busy with luggage until she had time to slip out.

If he got up early enough in the morning, he'd sit at breakfast until she came out. She couldn't miss breakfast. With that thought in his mind, he got into bed.

Unfortunately, he couldn't get to sleep right away. But he knew that his alarm was going to go off early, so he tried to think good thoughts. Jess would believe him. He just knew it.

JESSICA HAD A PLAN in place. Mary Jo had said she'd save Jessica some breakfast this morning. She stayed in her bed another fifteen minutes until after Jim knocked on her door. Then she got into the shower and dressed, braiding her hair down her back. She slipped into the kitchen and ate her breakfast. "Did he come through the kitchen?" she asked Mary Jo.

"Yes. And he wasn't happy."

"He banged on my door before he left."

"He's determined. What are you going to do?"

"I'm going to avoid him."

"Good luck—and don't tell me your plans. I don't want to have to lie to him."

"I won't. Thanks, Mary Jo."

She slipped out the back door, and with her hat in her hand, she strode toward the barn.

She grabbed a bridle from the tack room and went out into the pasture to catch Buck. When she led him back to the barn, Hank came over. "What are you doing?"

"Going for a ride."

"Did you talk to Jim?"

"No."

"But he wants to explain about that lady kissing him. She's an old girlfriend."

She ignored him and went to the tack room for her saddle and blanket and proceeded to suit up her horse.

"Where are you going?" Hank asked her.

"Out."

"Why aren't you telling me where you're going?"

"Because Jim is going to ask you. And you won't lie to him."

"I might. If you gave me enough reason."

She ignored him. When she swung up into the saddle, he grabbed her horse's bit.

"Turn us loose, Hank."

"But—"

She jerked her reins and Buck obeyed. She rode away from the barn. Knowing her brother was watching her, she intentionally rode toward the south. Then, after she reached some trees, she tracked back to the north.

She had a lunch Mary Jo had packed for her, as well as her canteen. And she carried a rifle in her saddle holster, just in case she came across a bear. There was no need for her to come back until after dinner had started.

She had to be there for after dinner. She was having game night tonight. But she could just appear when it was ready to start and she'd make sure she had people around her.

Anything to keep Jim away. He was—

Buck reared, catching her by surprise, and she went down hard on the left side of her body. Her reins were yanked out of her hands and Buck ran toward the stables.

She was alone, a long way from the ranch, and her arm hurt badly.

Chapter Eleven

After searching the house, Jim went to the barn. He found Hank there. "Have you seen your sister?"

"Yeah. She left on Buck about an hour ago."

"Where was she going?"

"She wouldn't tell me."

"Damn! I've been looking all over for her."

"I guess she didn't want to talk to you."

"She has responsibilities! She can't just run off."

Hank rolled his eyes. "Yeah. I'm going to be careful from now on. I don't want to mess up like Pete and Jessie."

Jim let out a big sigh. "She didn't mess up. At least not much. I'm the one in trouble, I guess. But I can't clear things up until I talk to her."

"I'll let you know when she comes in."

"Thanks, Hank."

He turned to walk back up to the house when one of the cowboys yelled. Turning around to see what was going on, he saw a saddled horse racing for the barn. It took him a minute to identify the horse as Buck. Then he raced back to the barn.

"That's Jess's horse! What happened?"

"I don't know," Hank said, moving into the pasture as Jim followed.

By the time they reached the horse, several cowboys were there, trying to calm him.

"Isn't this the horse Jessie usually rides?" one of the cowboys asked.

"Yeah, she left on him this morning," Hank replied. "Where did he come from?"

"From the north, it looked to me," another cowboy said.

"Let's saddle up and go find her!" Jim ordered.

"Wait! She went to the south. I watched her."

"She probably doubled back if she thought you'd tell me where she went. I'm betting we go to the north, but you can send a couple of men to the south to satisfy your mind."

"Okay, Jim, I'll go with you. Rob, you and Jamie go to the south. We'll shoot three times when we find her."

They all raced back to the barn to saddle up and set out in search of Jessica.

Jim scanned the land anxiously, but he saw nothing.

"She's been gone for about an hour, so she must've ridden at least half an hour, maybe more. Buck was pretty lathered up."

Jim didn't know if Hank was talking to himself or to him. "We need to find her as soon as possible."

"Yeah," Hank said with a worried look on his face. "I don't want to face Granddad and tell him Jessie is lost."

JESSICA COULDN'T BELIEVE she'd been thrown by her horse. Buck had been startled by a rattler, and her mind hadn't been on her riding but on her problems. It took awhile before she could get upright. Her shoulder and arm hurt like the dickens, but she knew she had to get up.

She could bear the pain as long as she held her left arm with her right one. It produced an awkward gait, and she didn't make it far before she had to rest.

"At this rate, I won't get back before sundown!"

Starting again, she followed the trail she'd ridden with Buck. She hoped her horse would go back to the house. That was her only hope of rescue. And at this point, she'd accept rescue from anyone. Even Jim.

She was still shielded by the trees when she heard horses. Though there shouldn't be anyone on the property but people she could trust, she didn't know whether to hail them or hide.

Reluctantly, she stood her ground. "Hey!" she yelled. The horsemen came toward her.

When she recognized Jim and Hank, she sobbed briefly in relief. But she was composed by the time they got close.

"Hi," she managed to say, standing there, covered

in dirt, tear streaks down her dirty face. She didn't care. She just wanted to be rescued.

Jim swung down from his horse as he stopped. Hank was right after him.

"Are you all right?" Jim asked.

"No. Not exactly."

"Where are you hurt?" Hank asked.

"I landed on my shoulder. I don't know if I broke something or what, but it's pretty painful."

"Okay, let's get you back to the house. Can you swing— No, I guess you can't." Jim stood there thinking a minute. "I know. Let me put you in the saddle. Then I'll get up behind you."

"I'd rather ride with Hank."

"Too bad. You're stuck with me."

"But—"

Hank spoke up. "I think you'd better ride with Jim. His horse is bigger than mine."

She glared at her brother. How insensitive could he be?

Jim led his horse to her. Then he said, "Sling your leg over the saddle when I lift you."

"No, I—"

He ignored her protest and put his hands around her waist and tossed her atop the saddle. She realized how strong he was, but the motion hurt her. Then he took her foot out of the stirrup, an automatic reaction for her, and put his own foot in and swung up behind her.

"Scoot up a little, Jess."

She had to do as he asked. It was the least she

could do. His arms went around her, gently cradling her, and he started his horse back toward the house.

"I've got to signal the others," Hank warned. To Jessica's surprise, her brother fired off three successive shots.

"Why did you do that?" she asked, her voice wobbly.

"To tell the others that we've found you. They were checking things out to the south, where you rode off. I was watching."

He sounded very put out with her, and Jessica couldn't handle retribution right now. She remained silent.

"Am I hurting your arm?" Jim asked.

"It hurts no matter what I do."

"Lean back and brace yourself against my chest. It might make the ride easier."

As much as she thought she didn't want to touch Jim, his suggestion gave her some support and did make the ride bearable. Most of the time.

By the time they reached the barn, a crowd had gathered, watching for their return. She was beyond speech. The pain was getting worse, despite her leaning against Jim.

Since her grandfather was one of the group, she whimpered, "Granddad, take me to the doctor."

Jim swung down from the right side of his horse and took hold of her waist. She knew he did that for her. It was easier to brace herself with her good shoulder, but even that hurt. He picked her up in his arms without asking and started toward her grandfather. "You drive. I'll hold her."

Cliff pulled his keys from his pocket. "Follow me."

Jessica wanted to protest. She didn't want Jim to go with them. But she was in too much pain to protest.

Her grandfather drove quickly to the doctor's office in Steamboat Springs. The doctor, when he realized Cliff was there again, laughed and asked if he was going for a group rate.

Jessica didn't laugh.

Jim carried her into an examining room. The doctor told the nurse to put her in a hospital gown and have the arm and shoulder X-rayed. All three men left the room.

As gentle as the nurse was, Jessica started crying again. She hated to be a crybaby, but it was so painful.

"I'm sorry. I know I'm hurting you, but we have to X-ray it to see what's wrong."

"It's—it's all right," she gasped.

When the nurse had her lie back on the bed, Jessica drew a breath of relief.

"Now, I'm going to bring the X-ray machine in here and you can just stay here, relaxed, while I take some pictures."

Jessica gave a muted hysterical laugh as the nurse left the room. She didn't feel that much more comfortable lying on the examining table than she'd felt out in the woods.

The nurse came right back with a big machine. "Now, take a deep breath and hold it."

She took several pictures and then wheeled the machine out of the room.

Lying there, knowing something was wrong, she of course thought the worst. Pete was already out of commission. How could she do such a stupid thing? How could she risk the running of the dude ranch? Oh, that's right! she thought. Jim's in charge, not her!

The doctor came in, wearing a serious expression. "Jessica, you've dislocated your shoulder. I think I can pop it back into place, but it will be painful. Then you'll need to wear a sling for several days."

"That's all?" she asked, stunned. So much pain and just a couple of days' recovery time? "Okay."

He took hold of her shoulder and did a quick snap. She almost passed out from the pain.

"The nurse is going to come dress you now and we'll put a sling on and give you a pain pill. It will all seem better soon."

Once the pill entered her system, she felt so much better. In time, she felt relaxed, tired. Pretty soon she didn't have a care in the world. Everything was wonderful…

When the nurse led her into the waiting room, Jim jumped up. "What did you do to her? She seems pretty out of it."

The nurse explained the procedure and gave him instructions for dispensing her pain medication.

Jim picked her up and started for the car. Cliff took the pills and the instruction sheet.

Back in the car, Jessica curled up in Jim's lap, laying her head on his shoulder, and closed her eyes.

When Jim started to get out of the car, she found her sleep disturbed. She woke up and smiled. "Where are we?"

"We're home, little girl," Cliff said.

"She's not aware of much, Cliff," Jim said. "I'll take her to her room. Maybe you can get Leslie to come help her."

"Yeah, sure, I'll do that."

When Jim put Jessica on her bed, she grabbed hold of him with her good arm. Still smiling, she said, "Don't go."

"Baby, I have to. You're not rational right now, but I have to be."

Leslie came in then, so Jim asked her, "Can you help Jess get undressed?"

He left the room. He couldn't take the temptation.

THOUGH THE TWO PILLS the doctor sent home with Jessica weren't as strong as the first one, she spent the next twenty-four hours in a fog. She didn't remember what she'd said or done until she woke up Wednesday morning. She shifted and discovered that her shoulder still ached.

But it wasn't as bad as it had been. She suddenly heard her door open. Jim tiptoed to her bed, not aware that she was awake.

"What are you doing coming into my room?" she demanded sharply.

"I didn't want to wake you if you were still asleep. How are you feeling?"

"Sore!"

"Do you need help getting dressed?"

She stared at him in outrage. "Not by you!"

"I was going to suggest I get Mary Jo if you need help. I haven't undressed you even once since you got hurt."

"I should hope not!" she exclaimed.

"Not that I'd object, you understand, but we've tried to preserve your dignity."

"Just get Mary Jo," she snapped.

"Your wish is my command. Can I have my morning kiss?"

"No!" But he said that as if it had been a habit. What had she done? She'd been angry when she fell. Had she forgotten her anger? Then she remembered the woman he kissed and all the anger flooded back.

She lay there waiting for Mary Jo. Suddenly she remembered that she'd promised to take over the cooking today. Just then, Mary Jo opened the door.

"Mary Jo, I just remembered I promised you the day off! I'm so sorry! Once I get up, I'll try—"

"Don't be silly. I knew you wouldn't be able to work today so one of my helpers is filling in for me."

"I'm so sorry to get you up early. You could've slept in."

"Jessica, I was already up. Let me help you get dressed and put your sling on. Then we'll go have breakfast together."

Half an hour later, they walked through the kitchen with greetings from the kitchen staff. Jessica stopped to thank Edith for taking over the kitchen. "You'll receive an additional increase in your check, Edith. I appreciate it."

"I'm glad to do it, Jessie."

Mary Jo fixed Jessica's plate and her own and led her to an empty table.

Jessica waited for Mary Jo to eat. Truth to tell, she didn't have much of an appetite this morning.

Suddenly, Jim was beside her. He pulled out a chair and sat down.

"I'd rather you go away," she said, her throat constricting with panic.

"I'm not going to go away. I've been waiting for three days to explain what happened when my ex-girlfriend greeted me so enthusiastically on Sunday."

"Are you sure she's an ex?" Jessica said stiffly.

"Yeah, I'm sure. We were together a couple of years. But I decided I didn't want to live in New York the rest of my life. I told her about my decision and she told me I was crazy. I ended our relationship before I even found the job. I left town without seeing her again. As far as I'm concerned, I want it to stay that way."

"What does she want?"

"She wants me to come back to New York City."

"You'd make more money." She hated to point out the benefits to his return to his old life, but she wanted to be sure he'd made the decision he wanted.

"I have quite a lot saved, Jess. And I can breathe. That's more important than money."

"You really mean it?"

"I don't ever intend to go to New York City again. Unless my wife wants to visit it."

"You have a wife?" She lowered her eyes.

"Not yet."

She looked up at him. "I overreacted. I'm sorry."

"If you'd listened to me right away, we could've cleared it up before you hurt yourself."

"I—"

She never finished her sentence, because her grandfather entered and immediately came over. "How are you, little girl?"

"I'm doing much better, thanks, Granddad."

"Did Jim explain everything to you?"

"No, I haven't yet. Mary Jo says that Edith can probably cook on Sundays so Mary Jo can have one more day off," Jim clarified for Jessica.

"That sounds great," Jessica replied.

"So everything is okay?"

She didn't know what to say.

Jim took over. "We're working on it."

"Okay. Leslie will be glad to hear it. She was worried about you, Jessie."

"That's nice of her."

"Yeah. She's a sweet lady," Cliff said, his eyes lighting up as he thought about Leslie.

"You'd better go get your food, Cliff," Mary Jo said.

"Yeah, I will." He wandered over to the buffet.

"He's got it bad, doesn't he?" Jim asked with a grin.

Jessica didn't say anything. She certainly wasn't going to make fun of her grandfather.

"Don't worry. I think he's safe with Leslie," Jim whispered.

"I hope so."

They ate in silence for several minutes. Then Jessica got up her nerve to resume their earlier conversation. "When I—"

But she was cut short again. This time by a high-pitched female voice. "Jim, sweetie, you beat me here!" Bronwyn said, and threw her hands around Jim's neck and kissed him on the cheek. "Save my place. I'll be right back."

Chapter Twelve

Jim shot a hand out to grab Jessica. "You're not going anywhere. Stay here and listen to me tell her I'm not interested."

"Why should I?"

"The last time you ran, you ended up hurting yourself. I don't want that again."

She didn't, either. But it was difficult to sit there calmly eating when that woman was coming back.

When Bronwyn brought her tray to the table, she sat down opposite Jim. Giving him a sunny smile, she said, "It's a beautiful day, isn't it?"

Ignoring her question, he replied, "Do you remember our discussion on Sunday, Bronwyn?"

"I don't give up easily, Jim. I'm still going to convince you to come back to New York."

"No, you're not. Look around you. Why would I want to leave this to return to New York?"

"Really, Jim, this is nice for a vacation, but you'll get bored in a week or two." She turned to Jessica. "Won't he?"

"I wouldn't know. I've lived here all my life and I'm not bored."

"You mean you haven't ever traveled?" Bronwyn asked in mock horror.

Jessica took a bite of her eggs and chewed them deliberately.

Jim glared at his former girlfriend. "Leave her alone!"

"Oh, yes, I forgot. She's the one chasing after you, isn't she?"

"No, she's not. It's the other way around."

Jessica continued to eat, though the eggs were sticking in her throat. But she had no intention of entering the argument going on in front of her.

The other three members of Bronwyn's group came in then and sat down at the next table. "Hey, Bronwyn, aren't you going to join us?" one of the men called out.

"Later, Deke. I'm visiting with Jim right now."

"Are you ready, Jess?" Jim said.

"Yes, but I can't carry my tray."

"I've got it."

When he walked away from the table, Bronwyn said to Jessica, "You'd better accept that he's going to leave. I won't give up. And in the end, I'll win."

Jessica said, "I don't try to make Jim's decisions for him. You should try that sometime." Then she got up and went to meet Jim as he was returning to the table.

"Is everything all right?" he asked.

"Of course. I'm sorry I reacted as I did on Sunday. That was juvenile of me."

"Come on, Jess, it wasn't that bad. I knew you were upset but—"

"Just because I wanted some time to myself didn't mean I was jealous!"

She tried to turn away, but he caught her good arm. "Come on. Let's go where we'll have some privacy."

He pulled her after him into the kitchen and then into the hall with their bedrooms. Opening the door to his room, he led her to his bed. "Sit down."

"Why should I?"

"Because I'm tempted to turn you over my knees."

"How dare you!"

"I dare because I rode out to find you when your horse came back. I dare because I carried you on my horse all the way back. I dare because I went to the hospital with you and held you all the way there and back. I dare because I've kissed you and told you how sorry I was at least ten times. I dare—"

"You what?" she demanded her brow furrowed.

"I said I've kissed you and apologized for my transgressions."

"I don't remember that!"

"I know. I took advantage of your…state. I'll confess to that. But you didn't seem to mind."

"I wasn't fully alert!"

"Maybe not. But you certainly didn't resist." He grinned at her.

"You're bragging about it?" she demanded in outrage.

"Honey, it did a lot for me. I'd begun to give up hope."

That gave her pause. "Hope for what?"

"For you to love me," he said simply.

He leaned over and kissed her lips softly. "Is that so bad?" he asked.

"No. But—"

He kissed her again.

"You shouldn't— I mean, we shouldn't—"

"What?"

"Do that."

"Why not?"

"Because I don't want to—to mislead you."

"How would you be misleading me?"

He kissed her again, this time a little deeper, and her lips clung to his. Her arms stole around his neck as he continued to kiss her. She couldn't resist him.

When he lifted his lips, she pulled him back to kiss her again.

The next time he pulled away, he said, breathing deeply, "I think we'd better stop right here. We're on a bed, in case you haven't noticed."

"Are we?" she asked, not thinking too clearly.

"Honey, I want to make love to you. I've been dying to make love to you, but not until you're ready."

"What? No, not—not yet."

He stood up and let his hand linger on her leg as long as he could. "Let me know when you're ready. I'll be waiting."

WHEN JESSICA GOT UP the next morning, she found her arm was much better. She got dressed by herself, even strapped on her sling. Then she took some over-the-counter pills to ease the pain a little.

She found Mary Jo in the kitchen. "How did yesterday go?"

"Not bad. I actually got to ride in the afternoon, with the better riders. It was fun. Of course, it made me a little sore this morning."

"That will improve if you keep at it."

"I know."

They smiled at each other, then Jessica went into the dining room to have breakfast. Just as she remembered that she couldn't hold her plate and serve herself at the same time, Jim called her name. She turned around.

"Good morning, sweetheart. I'll get your breakfast. Just sit down here with these nice people."

She remembered the two couples from registering them on Sunday.

"We heard about your accident. Is it very painful?" one woman asked.

"No, it's much better this morning. The doctor said I probably wouldn't have to wear my sling more than a week."

"That's a relief. What caused you to fall?"

"I wasn't paying attention when my horse reared. He was startled by a snake and I was thinking about…other things. You should never do that when you're riding."

"That's true," Jim said as he set a plate in front of Jessica. Then he bent and kissed her.

"Jim, not here!"

"They don't mind. I've already told them that I've fallen for you."

Her cheeks burned as she ducked her head.

"You can see I've still got some work to do." Jim chuckled as he watched Jess.

"Oh, I think she'll give in to you, Jim. You're so handsome."

"Hmm, I've always heard handsome is as handsome does," he returned.

Jessica had nothing to say.

After breakfast, Jim asked, "Do you want to go back to bed or maybe take a walk down to the corral?"

"I think I napped too much yesterday. I'd like to walk down to the corral."

"Good. Lean on me if you need to."

"Thank you, but I think I'll be all right."

"You could lean, anyway. It would feel good to me," he said with a teasing laugh.

"Maybe, a little."

They strolled out to the corral, and when they got there, he helped her climb up on the fence. He had just sat beside her when she heard a voice call out his name.

"Jim! Over here!"

They looked out to see Bronwyn was on one of the horses in the corral. He waved to her. Then he looked at Jessica. "I didn't know she'd be here."

"That's all right. You're with me, not her."

He smiled. "That's right, because that's where I want to be."

Bronwyn was paying more attention to Jim than she was her horse, an older plodding animal they were using for beginners. When the horses in the corral began a trot, Bronwyn almost fell off. She shrieked and pulled on the reins, causing a traffic jam in the corral.

The cowboy in charge had them all stop. Then he looked at Bronwyn. "Ma'am, is something wrong?"

"I—I didn't know you were going to speed up."

"Please pay attention. We don't want anyone hurt."

"I will," she said, obviously feeling insulted.

Jessica couldn't hold back a smile. She happened to look at Jim at that moment and he returned her amusement.

"She hates it when someone laughs at her."

"That must make it hard for her to try anything new."

"Yeah."

"You know, when you're trying to ski they say you're not learning if you're not falling."

Jim chuckled. "I'd suggest that to her if I weren't afraid she'd come back in winter. I don't want her here."

"Well, we're in agreement there."

"Yeah. Why were you so ready to believe I'd been leading you on?"

She didn't answer.

"Jess?"

She felt ready to tell him what had happened, what had made her so skittish. "I had a serious relationship in college. At least that's what I thought. I found out he had two of us going at once. When you said what you did about Pete and Mary Jo, I thought you were a good man. I lost control when it looked like you were two-timing me."

"I would never do that to you."

"Yes, I realized that…a little too late."

"I love you, Jess. I knew I was attracted to you when I saw you, but I didn't know your heart then. But I've come to know your bright mind, your determination, your love of life. You're the one that fits me like a glove."

She chuckled. "I've never been compared to a glove."

"Well, maybe I'm not so good with the words, but you're the one for me. I knew I didn't want to live in New York the rest of my life. When Bronwyn made it clear that she wouldn't consider a move, I breathed a sigh of relief.

"Then when I came here, it was as if my lungs were breathing deeper. And you were everywhere I looked. And I liked what I saw."

"Oh, Jim," Jessica said with a sigh, "you're saying some very sweet things."

Bronwyn called him again, but he ignored her, instead lowering his lips to Jessica.

When he lifted his mouth from hers, she said, "I think you'd better answer Bronwyn. She seems to be having trouble."

"I don't care," he whispered to her, keeping his gaze on her.

"I'm going to be a pain with this sling on for a few more days."

"I'll take care of you."

"You don't have anything else to do?"

"I'm driving the bus to Steamboat Springs tonight for some night life. Will you go with me?"

"I'd love to."

"Good. I was counting on it."

He kissed her again.

THAT NIGHT, AS JESSICA HAD felt sure would happen, Bronwyn and her friends were signed up for the Steamboat Springs trip. Jim asked some people to move out of the seat behind him on the bus and put Jessica there by herself. When Bronwyn and her friends got on, she took the first seat on the right side of the bus, opposite Jessica. Then she directed one of the men to sit by Jessica.

Jim was standing by the door and was distracted by other people boarding, but when he realized Deke was sitting by Jessica, he took the steps up into the bus. "You'll need to move, Deke. Jess is riding alone tonight."

"Why can't I ride here?"

"Because I want her to have room for her arm and not be crowded. There are other seats. Please move."

"I don't see why I should."

"Either move or don't go with us. It makes no difference to me which one you choose."

"I'm afraid you're rather crowding me. I think it

would be better if you moved," Jessica said with a sweet smile.

"I'm sorry. I didn't realize that. I'll be glad to give you more room."

He swung into the seat behind her, beside his friend Dub.

Jim closed the bus door and sat behind the wheel.

When they got off the bus a while later, they went to one of the local bars that played music and had dancing.

Jim wrapped his arm around Jessica as she got down from the bus, the last person to emerge.

"I smell a ploy by Bronwyn. Don't accept a dance with those guys with her."

"All right."

"That simple? Thanks, honey. I thought I'd have a fight on my hands."

She shook her head. "I don't want to dance with either of them. Especially if I can dance with you."

"I'm at your service, Jess. Anytime."

He ducked his head to kiss her.

She met him halfway, finding his kisses to be addictive.

Inside, the bar was hot and had a lot of smoke down at one end.

"I think the smokers are over that way. Let's sit over here," Jim said. He found an empty table for four. One of the couples from the bus, a couple that Jessica had talked to before, asked if they could join them.

"Of course. That would be nice," Jessica said.

The music started up again.

"Do you want to dance?" Jim asked.

"Let's wait until they play a slow song. I don't want to dislocate my shoulder again."

"I'm with you," said Janis, the older woman sitting with them. She and her husband, Scott, were pleasant companions.

Jessica and Janis were talking when someone tapped her on her good shoulder.

"Want to dance?" Deke asked.

"No, thank you."

"Why?"

"Because I don't care to," Jessica replied kindly.

Janis, sitting on the other side of Jim, nudged him. He'd been discussing something with her husband. When he looked at her, she pointed to the man at Jessica's shoulder.

"What do you want, Deke?"

"I want to dance with this lady."

"No." Jim was emphatic.

Deke didn't accept his word. "I think she should answer for herself."

"I already did," Jessica interjected. "No, thank you."

"So go away, Deke," Jim said.

"I'm tired of you bossing me around."

"You should be used to it. I was your boss in New York."

"You're not my boss now."

"Maybe not, but you chose to come here. I didn't ask you to come."

"You think I did? It was Bronwyn who told us it would be fun."

"She was wrong."

"Yeah, tell me about it! I'm ready to go home."

"Suit yourself," Jim drawled, giving him a straight look.

Deke stalked across the floor.

The music changed to a ballad and Jessica looked at Jim. "Want to dance?"

"I've been waiting," he assured her, rising to pull her to her feet. "I'll need to wrap both arms around you, since you can't hang on. Is that okay with you?"

"Oh, yes," she said with a sigh as she rested her head on his shoulder and pressed against him.

His arms held her close as they moved slowly to the music. Jessica kept her eyes closed, leaving the direction to him. They moved as if they'd danced together forever.

"Hey, you two are good together," Scott said.

"Thanks," Jim said,

Jessica just smiled, never opening her eyes.

AS EXPECTED, BRONWYN CAME to ask Jim to dance, but he refused. She accused him of being rude, but he just smiled and said nothing else.

Finally she stomped off to the other side of the room.

When Jim decided most of the people who'd come with them were ready to go home, he called for his passengers to be on the bus in ten minutes.

"We aren't ready to leave yet," Bronwyn announced with a slight slur.

"That's up to you. If we leave you here, it's up to you to get back to the ranch. And you'd better not make a lot of noise and disturb your neighbors' sleep."

Bronwyn was still complaining, but her friends told her they were going back. She finally got on the bus, grumbling as she had to take a back seat because the front ones were all filled.

Jessica sat in the seat behind Jim, thinking about her day with him, his care of her, his sweet-talking. He'd won her over. She'd known he'd be able to. She'd tried to protect her heart, but he was too good to ignore.

When the bus stopped in front of the main building of the Lazy L, Jessica didn't move. She knew Jim would have to park the bus near the barn. They could go in by the back door.

After Jim had parked, he led Jessica down the steps. "Think we'll be locked out?"

She held out a key she had hidden in her sling. "I believe in being prepared."

"Good girl. I didn't think of that."

They slipped in the back door, being as quiet as they could. It wouldn't do to wake up the others. Especially with what Jessica had planned.

When they reached her door, he bent to wrap his arms around her and kiss her. After several minutes, she turned out of his arms. "It's late."

"Yeah, I know. I shouldn't have kept you out so long."

"I think I'll need help to get out of my sling," she said.

Jim frowned. "You want me to wake up Mary Jo?"

"That doesn't seem fair. Can't you help me?"

Jim frowned even more. "I—I guess I could, but what are you asking?"

"I want you to come in."

"Okay, I'll help you."

"Good." She opened her door and led him in. Then she closed the door.

Stepping up against him, she said, "Will you kiss me?"

"Oh, honey, I want to kiss you, but it might be dangerous here. I mean, we're in your bedroom."

"I know. But I think we can handle it."

"Okay." Jim reached out for her. "Let me remove your sling for you."

"Oh, I can do that," she said, taking the sling off. "I just wanted you in here."

"Why?"

She closed the gap between them. "Because I want you to make love to me."

Chapter Thirteen

I want you to make love to me.

They were words she thought she'd never utter again. But she had. To Jim. And she meant them.

Jim, apparently had trouble believing her. He took a deep breath. "Are you sure? I don't want to pressure you."

"I think *I'm* pressuring you."

He smiled at her. "Well, then, I guess I'll just have to do what you want!"

He took her in his arms, lowering his lips to hers. After a long kiss, he said, "I love your lips. They're so soft."

"I love your lips, too," she told him, seeking them again.

It had been so long since she'd given her body to a lover. It took a lot of courage for her to do so now. But this man inspired her to commit to him. She knew he really believed what he'd said to her brother Pete.

Purposefully she unbuttoned his shirt, seeking to

stroke his chest. In turn, he helped her remove her clothes. Their hands seemed to be everywhere on each other's bodies, stroking, touching, exploring. They stretched out on the bed, all their clothes now thrown on the floor, as they enjoyed each other's bodies. Each touch led to another one, each bringing pleasure.

Jessica hadn't remembered making love like this. She felt his erection against her belly, larger than she'd expected. He seemed ready to explode. Excitement built in her, meeting his level. She wanted to share in the ultimate satisfaction.

When he entered her, after putting on the condom that she'd stolen from her brother Pete, he moved in and out until she thought she'd burst into little pieces. Until, finally, she thought she had.

"Oh, Jim!" she exclaimed.

"Are you all right?" he asked, his voice low.

"Oh, yes! I'm wonderful."

"Yeah, me, too."

They lay breathless on the bed, in each other's arms, their legs intertwined. After a few minutes, Jim reached for the sheet and blanket to cover them. He ran his fingers over her hair until she went to sleep.

Jim looked at the dark beauty as she lay against the pillow, gripped by a tenderness he'd never felt before. She inspired him to do better, to protect her, to care for her. If he was given the chance. He didn't want to rush her, but he definitely wanted to make their relationship a permanent one.

She stirred in her sleep and he held her closer.

Her scent filled his nostrils. He breathed deeply, thinking it was the most wonderful scent in the world—a trace of perfume and her.

He rested his head on the pillow next to her. Where he wanted to be the rest of his life.

BECAUSE OF THEIR LATE NIGHT, they both woke up long after daybreak. They each made a mad dash for the showers, which helped with the awkwardness of the "morning after." They hadn't talked much while they were making love and Jim didn't really know what she was thinking.

When they met at the breakfast table, he was relieved to see Jessica's smile. He greeted her with a light kiss, just to stake his claim. She didn't refuse him.

They sat together and ate breakfast. When they finished, she said, "What are you going to do today?"

"I've got to give Hank some support and check with the man Pete chose to handle the cattle operations. What about you?"

"I promised one of our guests last night that I'd give her a private riding lesson this morning. She has yet to ride because she's too frightened. I thought it would be a shame for her not to at least ride once while she's here."

"Okay, I'll look for you at lunch."

She smiled. "I'll look forward to it."

He gave her another kiss and reluctantly got up from the table.

Before Jessica could follow him, Bronwyn slid into the empty chair at her table.

"I want to talk to you."

"Why?"

"I want you to give Jim up."

"I don't see why I should."

"Because I'm pregnant."

Jessica stared at her. The expression on the woman's face convinced her it was the truth. She swallowed the pain that attacked her and asked, "Have you told Jim?"

"No. I want him to come back without having to force him. But if that's the only way I can win him back, then I will."

"I believe you should be honest with him. He doesn't want to come back to New York."

"Because of you!"

"No, I don't think it's because of me. He's a country boy at heart."

"He was happy in New York City!"

"Then why did he leave?"

"Because I broke up with him."

"I don't believe you."

"It's true. I told him I wasn't happy with him. He agreed to let me go. But I didn't know I was pregnant."

"I suggest you be honest with him," Jessica said again.

"No. I want to do it my way."

"You have twenty-four hours to tell him. Then I'll tell him."

"Damn you! Can't you just give him up?"

"No."

Bronwyn got up and walked away.

Jessica's serene happiness from last night disappeared. How could Jim make love to her if he'd left a woman pregnant in New York?

Last night, she'd made sure she had a condom. She didn't want to risk having sex without protection. Why hadn't Jim taken that precaution with Bronwyn?

And she'd been stupid enough to promise not to tell. So she had to avoid him.

How could she do that? He was meeting her for lunch. And then there was tonight. She'd planned on having Jim in her bed again. She *wanted* him in her bed. What was she going to do?

She felt heartsick. But she'd given her word. Twenty-four hours and she'd be free. Twenty-four hours and she'd know what Jim was going to do.

She didn't want to give him up.

JIM HAD A BUSY MORNING. He found Pete down at the barn, talking to the man he'd selected to handle the cattle operation. Jim stepped forward and joined their conversation.

"How are things going, Pete?"

"Fine. I was just telling Andy what I wanted him to do today. We're going to drive a herd to a new pasture. We've got some dudes who've asked to participate. We're going to give them the job of drag, you know, bringing up the rear."

"Yeah, I know. How long will that take?"

"Probably four or five hours."

"Do you need more help?" Jim asked. "I can ride with you if you do."

Andy jumped at his offer. "Do you mind? I'd feel more comfortable with that inexperienced bunch if you were along."

"Sure. I just need to give a message to Jess."

"I can give her a message. What is it?" Pete asked.

"Just tell her I won't be in for lunch."

"Sure, I can do that."

"Thanks." Jim excused himself to saddle a horse and ride out with Andy. He liked what he'd seen of the young man. He guessed he'd get a closer look today.

But he hated missing lunch with Jess. He'd been looking forward to tasting her lips again. Oh, well, he'd make up for it tonight.

That was comforting. He could look forward to holding her against him, making love to her, sleeping with her. For the first time in his life, he felt he'd found a place where he could be happy.

With Jess.

JESSICA GAVE JANIS HER riding lesson. It went well, but since Janis and her husband were leaving Sunday, she didn't fool herself that she'd made a difference in Janis's life.

Because she'd promised to keep Bronwyn's secret, she walked to lunch with Janis, hoping she'd join her. Her husband, Scott, came in at the same time and the three of them went in to lunch. Jessica was watching for Jim when Pete, on his crutches, stopped by her table.

"You're not wearing your sling?" he asked.

"No, I'm doing much better. How are you?"

"Still hobbling around. Oh, Jim asked me to give you a message."

"What?" she asked, tensing up.

"He wanted you to know that he couldn't come to lunch. He's riding with Andy, moving a herd, and won't be back until this evening."

"All right. Thanks, Pete. Do you want to join us?"

"Sure." He turned to the couple at the table. "Hi, I'm Pete, Jessie's brother."

"Yes, we heard you had an accident. How long will you be on crutches?" Janis asked.

"Another four or five weeks."

"That's too bad," Janis said.

"Yeah, but it's my own fault."

Jessica's head came up. She couldn't believe her brother wasn't blaming his accident on Mary Jo. That was a change of attitude!

"How's Mary Jo doing?" he asked after a minute.

"Fine. She's promoted one of her workers to assistant chef and she's doing the cooking on Wednesdays and Sundays."

"Good."

Jessica didn't want to discuss his change of attitude in front of the others. But she did want to talk to him. When lunch was over, she asked, "Pete, can I talk to you a minute?"

"Sure. I was just going down to the barn to try to help Hank."

"I'll walk with you."

"Okay."

They got outside and she said, "I was glad to hear you say that your injury was your own fault. You're not blaming Mary Jo for your broken leg?"

"No."

"Have you said that to her?"

"No."

"Why not?"

"She won't let me near her."

"Do you blame her?"

He shrugged.

Not quite the answer she'd hoped for, but it was a start. "Well, good luck with Mary Jo. And with taking care of things."

"Thanks."

They had reached the corral.

"I think I'm going to sit and watch for a while," Jessica said. "Tell Hank to let me know if he needs me to do anything."

"I will."

Jessica climbed up on the top rail and watched some little children on their horses. That reminded her that she wanted Hank or Pete or Jim to find some ponies to stable for the children.

Maybe not Jim. He could be in New York soon, if

Bronwyn was telling the truth. She couldn't see Jim giving up his child. Maybe Bronwyn would give him the child if he didn't agree to come to New York.

Could she raise another woman's child?

If she were honest with herself, she wouldn't want that burden. She wanted to bear her own child. Jim's child.

She stopped herself. She'd deal with that problem when it arose.

The immediate problem was tonight. What was she going to do? Could she make some excuse to Jim that he'd believe? Did she want to? Maybe she should be honest with him. Tell him that they'd jumped too quickly to a sexual partnership.

Would he believe that when she'd practically begged him to make love to her?

But could she have sex with him knowing he may have made a baby with Bronwyn?

JIM FINISHED WITH THE cattle drive about four-thirty. He rode back to the barn with the dudes who'd helped with the move. They were all cheerful about their job, and Jim had to admit they'd held their own.

Being in the rear wasn't much fun for him. He could've contributed more if he'd ridden alongside the herd. But he supposed he'd have to say he'd done his job—no one had been hurt and all the guests had had fun.

Without having to worry about the cows, he'd had

a lot of time to daydream about Jessica. But he'd have to be careful or he'd have an accident like Jess.

He was anxious to see her. To touch her. He'd missed her today. Would she be hanging out at the corral? Or maybe she had taken a nap. She probably needed to.

Then she'd have enough energy for other activities.

A smile on his face got attention when he dismounted.

"Hey, Jim, what's so great that you're smiling like that?" Hank asked.

"Just pleasant thoughts," he said. "Have you seen Jess?"

"She was down here early in the afternoon, but I think she went back to the house about two or three. Do you need her for something?"

"No, I just wondered." He'd have to be careful or he'd start a lot of talk. Thinking about his behavior the past couple of days, he realized he'd probably already caused some talk.

Had Jess heard it? Was that why she wasn't waiting for him? She might've gotten upset if her brothers had teased her.

He rubbed down his horse after putting up his tack. Then he turned the horse out into the pasture. He'd been a good ride and deserved good treatment.

Then Jim strode to the house.

Jess was playing bridge with Leslie and two ladies. She said hello to him but indicated she couldn't talk. He guessed bridge took more concentration than horseback riding.

He noticed Jess looked a little tired. She must not have had a nap today. Would she not want to make love again tonight?

He decided to go to the kitchen for a snack, though it wasn't what he was hungry for.

He took an extra snack and went to find Pete, whom he knew was having a hard time right now.

"Thanks," Pete said, as he took the plate. He settled down in his chair and leaned the crutches against it. "I'm so bored. I stayed out most of the day, but there's only so much I can do."

"I know."

"But, you know, I have to give Jessie credit. She's been everywhere today. Out to the corral, down to one of the cabins that had a problem, checking on the guests. I used to think she had it easy."

Jim shook his head. "She doesn't. And she does a good job."

"Yeah. She seems to know everyone's name, too, without reading those name tags. I have to admit I fought her on a lot of that stuff. I just didn't think it was necessary."

Jim was glad to hear Pete coming around. He figured now was a good time to broach another subject. "Has she talked to you about the winter season?"

"No."

"Well, we've discussed staying open for a lot of the ski season. I think it's a good idea. We'd be closed October and November, then open December through

February. Closed for March and April and then start up again in May."

Before Pete could protest, he added, "You have to remember that you wouldn't be involved much. After all, you can't give rides in a snowstorm. We'd have them for breakfast, put them on a bus and pick them up in the late afternoon."

"You're assuming all of them will go skiing. What about the ones who are too tired to ski that day? Or don't ski at all? They'll just come along and expect someone to entertain them."

"You might be right about that, but I don't think you'd be responsible for entertaining them, unless your leg is still in a cast," he teased with a grin.

"Yeah, I guess. But that would mean that Mary Jo has to fix at least two meals a day, and some of these people expect a packed lunch so they don't have to spend money on a meal at lunch."

"That's true. I hadn't thought of that. But she's going to have four months off."

"You mean she won't cook at all? What will *we* eat?"

"What did you eat before Mary Jo came?"

"We had a cook while Jessie was at college. Then, when she came back, she took over the kitchen. I guess she could cook us lunch."

"I don't think that's a good plan. We may have to pay Mary Jo more to do the packed lunches. I'll have to talk to her about that."

"There's a lot involved in this business, isn't

there?" Pete said. After a minute, he said, "You know, Jim, you've done a good job. I'm sorry I was so difficult at first."

"That's all right. I knew all three of you were hurting, having lost your parents. Cliff was right that the blame could fall on me and let the three of you heal."

"You're not going to leave, are you?" Pete said sharply. "I know your old girlfriend is here, but you're not going back to New York City, are you?"

"Nope, I'm through with New York. I hope to stay here for a long time."

Just then, Leslie walked by.

"Leslie, is the bridge game over?" Jim asked.

"Yes. Jessica had to talk to a man whose wife is sick."

"What cabin?" Jim asked, standing.

"Three."

"I'll go check on her," he said.

Neither Pete nor Leslie said anything and Jim hurried out of the main house.

After he left, Leslie said, "He certainly works hard, doesn't he?"

"Yeah. And I'm beginning to think that might have to do with Jessie."

JESSICA STILL HADN'T COME up with a reason to avoid Jim. All day she'd worried about tonight. She decided to just be too tired. He'd leave her alone if she looked exhausted. So she'd spent most of the day running from one place to another.

Now she was going to check on a sick guest. That way she was out of the main house now that Jim had returned. Not that she knew enough medicine to determine much. But she could at least express sympathy.

She knocked on the door and waited for an answer. When the door opened, the woman, Angela, looked really ill.

"I'm sorry to bother you, but I wanted to see how you're doing."

"Thank you. I'm doing better."

"Why don't you sit down," Jessica said, smiling at the woman. "Did you have lunch?"

"No. It just didn't seem worth the walk. And I was throwing up, anyway. Some friends of mine had a bout of the flu just before we left. I guess I got it from them."

"Let me call Mary Jo, our chef, and see if she can make you some soup and have someone bring it to you. If you keep that down, maybe you can come to dinner."

She called the kitchen and explained to Mary Jo what she needed.

After she hung up the phone, she assured Angela that Mary Jo would have some soup down to her in no time.

"That's so nice of you."

"Where's your husband?"

"He stayed for an hour or two, but I told him to go ahead and ride this afternoon. There was no point in hanging around here to watch me make trips to the bathroom."

"That was very generous of you."

"Well, as much as we paid, he should get to enjoy it."

"I know." But Jessica thought she'd like someone to stay with her if she got sick. "I'll stay with you until you get your soup."

"You're so sweet. My husband should be back soon."

"Sometimes the rides take longer than planned, though."

"Don't you have to be back at the main lodge to do things?"

"No. At this time of the day, everything is about done. Just sit back and relax. I think that's the best medicine. To get enough rest."

"Yeah. I didn't get much rest when it started, but it seems to have calmed down. I actually had a nap this afternoon."

"Good. And did you do any activities that you liked?"

"Oh, yes, I started riding lessons on the first day. I'm really getting pretty good. And I enjoyed every meal. The food here is wonderful."

"Yes, our chef is very good."

A knock on the door caused Jessica to check her watch. That was really fast for the soup. "I'll get it," she told Angela.

When she opened the door, however, it wasn't someone from the kitchen. It was Jim.

Chapter Fourteen

"What are you doing here?"

"I thought I should check on you and our sick guest. Hello," he said over Jessica's shoulder.

"Hello," Angela responded. "That's very thoughtful of you."

Jessica shooed him away, trying to shut the door. "There's no need for you to come in. You don't want to get sick."

"I'll be all right." He stepped around Jessica.

"Mary Jo is sending some soup to settle her stomach."

As if on cue, a knock on the door interrupted them. Jessica opened the door and took a tray from one of the women from the kitchen. She carried it over to Angela.

"It's chicken noodle. I hope this helps."

"I'm actually hungry," Angela said, eager to try the soup.

"Good. If this stays down, you can come to dinner. I think we're having crepes tonight."

As Jessica spoke, the front door opened. Angela's husband, Joe, looked surprised when he entered.

"Is something wrong?"

"No, Joe, we were just visiting with your wife," Jessica explained, "and we got her some soup."

"Thanks. How are you feeling, honey?" He turned to his wife.

"We'll leave you two alone now," Jessica said. "Call if you need anything."

Jessica stepped outside, followed by Jim.

"That was thoughtful of you, Jessie."

"The poor woman was alone most of the day, with nothing to eat. It didn't take a lot of thought to think she'd like something to eat."

He walked alongside her, itching to touch her, but he sensed she wasn't as eager as he was. Something was wrong, but he didn't know what.

"Did you have a good day?"

"It was a bit tiring," she said.

"You didn't get a nap?"

"No. I think I'll go to bed early."

He liked that topic. Except the idea of going to bed early. It definitely sounded like she didn't want a guest.

"You don't want me to share your bed tonight?"

She gave him a quick look. Then she focused on the path. "I'm really tired, Jim. I don't think I'd be much fun tonight."

He knew he didn't need to be entertained. He just wanted to hold her if she wanted to go to sleep. But he didn't think she was interested. Obviously, she didn't feel about him the way he thought about her.

"You don't have to entertain me. It would just be nice to be with you."

"Maybe another night," she said without looking at him.

This morning she'd been loving and attentive. He left to go to work and when he came back, she wasn't interested. Something was wrong.

"Did something happen that I need to know about?"

"No, I don't think so."

She still wasn't looking at him.

"Did I do something to upset you?"

She looked at him then. "No, nothing."

So what was causing her disinterest? Because that's what it seemed like to him.

"So you're just tired?"

"Yes, I'm really tired."

He reached out to take her hand, and she jerked it away.

"So why don't you want me to touch you?" he asked quietly.

"Jim, I just need to be alone tonight, okay?"

"Okay." What else could he say when she wouldn't tell him what was wrong?

She whispered, "Thank you."

They walked alongside each other, keeping a distance that Jim hated.

When they got to the house, he opened the door.

She slipped past him and walked fast enough that he didn't try to catch her. What was the point?

JIM DIDN'T SIT BESIDE her at dinner.

Jessica chastised herself. That was what she'd wanted, wasn't it? She'd managed to chase him away. So why was she so depressed?

Because she wanted him with her every minute of every day. And especially the nights. But the little bomb Bronwyn had dropped on Jessica had made a difference.

She couldn't cling to him when he might have to be with Bronwyn. He didn't know yet, she could tell. If he'd known, he would've said something. Tomorrow she could talk to him, ask him what he was going to do. For now she could do nothing.

When Bronwyn sat down at his table, she thought maybe she was telling him now. Then she realized that wouldn't happen. She would want a private discussion to reveal her secret.

What if she, Jessica, were pregnant with his child? Even thinking about that made Jessica glow.

"Jessie? Are you all right?" her grandfather asked, staring at her.

"Yes, Granddad, I'm fine."

"Okay. Let me know if you need anything."

"I will."

When her grandfather joined Leslie, Jessica sighed. How weird that her grandfather had the right to join Leslie, and she didn't have the right to join Jim.

It wasn't fair.

Pete slid into the seat opposite Jessica. He was managing very well on his crutches.

In no time he asked after Mary Jo.

Jessica stared at her brother. "She's doing fine. Now that she gets Sunday and Wednesday off, I think she'll really do well. She went riding on Wednesday afternoon. She said she really enjoyed it."

"I didn't know."

"Yes, she was sore but enthusiastic."

After another pause, he asked, "Do you think she'll ever talk to me again?"

It was obvious to Jessica that her brother was hurting. But she didn't have a lot of sympathy for him. After all, he'd betrayed Mary Jo carelessly, as if she didn't matter. And she was Jessica's best friend.

"I don't know, Pete. You hurt her badly."

"I know."

He didn't say anything else. Jessica felt sorry for him, but she knew Mary Jo suffered a lot more.

When the meal was over, she had to start the evening's entertainment with Darrell, the cowboy who played his guitar and sang to the guests. He sometimes even invited the guests to join in the singing, which she thought was a fitting end to their visit.

Of course, that would also prevent Jim from approaching her. She was too busy. It also provided Bronwyn time to talk to him privately. Which she did.

When Jim broke away from her, Jessica thought

maybe Bronwyn had told him. She searched for Jim's response, but his face revealed nothing. He saw her looking at him and waved. She knew by that wave that Bronwyn hadn't told him.

Turning away, she moved to the front of the gathering audience.

"Good evening. As this is the last evening of your visit, I wanted to leave you with a touch of the West. Our resident entertainer will bring you a taste of the Old West with tunes he learned as a little boy, around the campfire and at home. Let me introduce you to Darrell, our resident singer."

Though she'd intended to withdraw early, she found herself staying to listen to the cowboy. When he finished, after several curtain calls, she thanked the audience for their participation all during their stay.

After she said good-night, she headed for her room. Jim, who had been watching the program, followed her. She ducked into the kitchen to chat with Mary Jo, but she wasn't there.

Jim caught up with her then. Facing him, she said, "I saw you talking to Bronwyn. Did she convince you to return to New York?"

"No. Why would you even think such a thing?"

"No reason. I just thought…"

"Is that what's bothering you?"

"Of course not. I just wondered if you discussed it."

"We didn't talk about me going back to New York. I've already told her that's not up for discussion."

"But in certain circumstances, you might find it

necessary," she suggested, peeking at him from beneath her lashes.

"I can't think of any circumstances."

"Well, I have to go to bed. I'll see you in the morning." She rushed into her room and closed the door.

He didn't even get a kiss? What had he done that was so terrible?

He went into his bedroom, puzzled by Jess's behavior. Something was seriously wrong.

THE NEXT MORNING IN THE dining room, Jessica saw Jim walk in with Bronwyn and her friends. From the looks of things, Bronwyn hadn't told him yet.

Then Bronwyn and Jim moved across the room to a private corner.

Finally, Jessica thought. Finally she was going to tell him. Watching them closely, she saw an angry response on Jim's face. At least now he knew why she'd withdrawn.

He stalked out of the dining room.

During their free time, after the guests had departed, Jessica waited for Jim to come talk to her.

With the time almost up, she decided to find him.

She knocked on his door, but there was no answer. She wandered back to the kitchen. "Edith, have you seen Jim?"

"Yes, he had breakfast in here. Then he said he was going out for a ride."

Jessica wandered out to the dining room again.

When she saw Jim come in, she beamed at him, an inviting smile on her face. When he saw that smile, he must have interpreted it correctly, as he hurried across the room to sit down next to her.

"Are you feeling better this morning?" he asked.

"Yes. How do you feel?"

"Glad you're better."

Oddly, he didn't seem upset about anything.

After a minute, she said, "So, Bronwyn told you?"

"Told me what?"

She stared at him. "About the baby, of course."

"What baby?"

"Your baby!" she said.

He looked at her blankly. "What are you talking about?"

"Bronwyn told me yesterday morning that she's pregnant with your baby. I promised to keep quiet about it until she had a chance to tell you."

"You're kidding!"

"No, I'm not!"

"Jess, Bronwyn didn't tell me anything about that. Is that why you didn't want me around last night?"

"It didn't seem right if Bronwyn was pregnant with your baby. Are you sure she didn't even hint about it?"

"No. Nothing."

"Are you sure you're— Could you not be the father?"

"I don't know. But I'm going to find out. I'll be gone a couple of days while I fly to New York to speak with Bronwyn. But I'll be back with a clear answer. Will you wait for me? I know I don't have any right to ask that, but I'm asking."

"Yes. I'll wait for your answer."

He bent down and kissed her before he went to speak to Cliff. She stared at him, wishing she could beg him to stay with her. But he needed to find the truth.

JIM GOT OFF THE PLANE, carrying an overnight bag. He was still dressed in jeans and boots, wearing a light jacket. He hailed a taxi, then headed for a hotel near where Bronwyn lived. After he got a room, hopefully for only one night, he walked to Bronwyn's apartment.

After knocking on her door, he waited there, hearing a masculine voice. She was living with someone?

When the door swung open, he had his answer. His old friend Deke was standing there.

"Jim? Are you coming back?"

"No, I'm not. I wasn't aware that you and Bronwyn were living together."

"I didn't know I had to check in with you before I made a move on your old girlfriend." Deke sounded defensive.

"May I come in, or are you going to leave me standing in the hall?"

"I'd like to…but I guess you'd better come in."

Jim stepped over the threshold. But he was re-membering things during his last month with Bronwyn that he hadn't understood at the time.

Deke stepped to the door leading into the bedroom. "Hon? You'd better come out here."

"What is it? I'm busy unpacking."

"Come here," Deke ordered.

Irritation on her face, Bronwyn came through the door. Deke pointed to Jim before she could say anything.

"Jim! I didn't know you'd changed your mind!" She looked pleased at seeing him.

"I haven't."

"Then why are you here?"

"I wanted to congratulate you on your pregnancy."

"She said she wouldn't tell you!"

"Only if you did tell me."

Deke interrupted. "Wait a minute. What are you two talking about?"

"Hasn't she told you she's pregnant? Strange, I would've thought you'd know about it first." Jim just stared at Bronwyn.

"We're having a baby? Honey, why didn't you tell me?"

"Because she told Jess it was my baby," Jim told him.

He stood quietly, watching the argument that broke out.

Finally, he stepped in. "Bronwyn, I need the truth. Is this my baby?"

"Yes. No. I don't know."

"How far along are you?"

After a quick look at Deke, she said, "Two months."

Jim hesitated before he said, "Then it's possible?"

She wouldn't look at him. But she also didn't look at Deke.

"So you were sleeping with both of us?" Jim asked.

"I had to do something! You were talking about leaving. If I didn't have someone else to go out on dates with, what would I do?"

"So I was a meal ticket, and you needed a replacement?"

"No, I love you, Jim, honestly."

"No, you didn't love me. You would've been too upset to date other men if you'd loved me."

She glared at him.

"I think it's my baby!" Deke said. "Yes, I was sleeping with her a lot more often than you!"

"Yes, I see. My question is, how do we prove it?"

"They can't do a test until the baby is born!" she snapped.

"Are you sure of that?" Jim asked.

"They can, but it might injure the baby. So I don't want the test until after the baby is born."

"So you'll have the test then?"

"Of course," she said, but she didn't look at him.

"Deke, can I trust you to have the test done?"

"Yeah. I want to know who the father is, too."

"Then you know where to reach me."

Jim left the apartment to go back to the hotel, angry about what had happened. Even angrier that he wouldn't know the truth until seven months from now.

JIM WOKE UP TO A ringing phone. He reached for the receiver while he looked at his watch in the dim light. "Hello?"

"Jim, it's Deke."

"Yeah, Deke, what is it?"

"We're at the hospital. It seems— Something is wrong with Bronwyn. She thinks she may be miscarrying."

"What hospital?"

"Lenox Hill."

"I'm on my way."

It was four in the morning and Jim thought it was a good thing you could always find a taxi in New York.

At the hospital, he joined Deke in the waiting room. They didn't talk much, until Deke decided he had to confess. "We had an argument, a big one. I accused her of trying to use the baby to get you back."

"I think that's probably true, but I don't know if the baby is mine. Bronwyn is an interesting woman, but I wouldn't call her trustworthy. You need to be careful."

"If she loses the baby, I don't think I want to go on with her. I mean, I didn't think about it earlier, but if she's determined to cheat on me, I don't know what I'd do."

"I know."

They sat there together, waiting for the doctor to come out. When he finally did, the news wasn't good. Bronwyn had lost the baby.

Deke approached him. "Can you tell which of us was the father?"

The doctor looked at them with an understanding eye. "The baby had B blood type, if that helps." Both Deke and Jim said thank-you.

"Would either of you like to see Bronwyn?" the doctor asked.

Jim refused, but Deke said he would see her.

Jim thought that was appropriate since, based on the blood type, Deke was the real father.

Chapter Fifteen

Jim didn't go back to sleep. He packed his bag and went to the airport to take the first flight to Denver. He didn't want to wait for anything.

All that mattered to him was getting back to Jess. Her attitude the past two days was easily explained now. And he could face her with an easy conscience.

He thought about holding her in his arms again. Had it only been three nights ago that he'd made love to her? It felt like weeks.

Would she welcome him to her bed again? He wasn't sure, but he certainly hoped so.

When the plane landed in Denver at noon, he called the ranch and talked to Leslie. "Tell Mary Jo I'll be there for dinner. And Jess, too."

"I will, Jim. We're glad you're coming back."

"Have you had any trouble?"

"No, Pete has run everything."

"Good. I'm anxious to get home."

JESSICA FELT LIKE A walking zombie. Jim had left Sunday as soon as he realized what Bronwyn had said. She didn't know if he'd return or if he'd feel differently about her.

She'd welcomed the new guests, but she didn't remember anything about them. Today she'd made several mistakes, not recognizing anyone. She finally apologized and explained that she had a headache. After that, she redoubled her efforts.

When she came in to lunch, she sat with Pete again. Her older brother was managing everyone, much to her surprise.

"How are you doing, Pete?" she asked.

"Better than I have since I broke my leg."

"I'm glad to hear that," she said, no enthusiasm in her voice.

"Jessica, there you are." Jessica turned at the sound of Leslie's voice. "Jim called and said he'd be here for dinner. He asked me to tell you." Leslie beamed at Jessica.

"Thank you, Leslie. I was afraid he might stay in New York, so it's good to hear he's coming back."

"You thought he might stay?" Leslie asked.

"I probably misunderstood," Jessica said with a weak smile.

When Leslie walked away, Pete said, "You didn't misunderstand. What caused you to think he might not come back?"

She couldn't bring herself to tell her brother the truth. "Some financial issue," she lied. Then, eager to get away, she made up an excuse about having to check with Mary Jo.

She wandered into the kitchen. "Mary Jo, did you hear that Jim will be back for dinner?"

"Yes, Leslie told me. I'm glad."

"Me, too."

Mary Jo sent her friend a grin. "Yes, that's no surprise."

"What are you talking about?"

"Come on, Jessica, everyone saw him kissing you. I hope things will work out for you."

Too nervous to think about that, Jessica felt the need to ride, to feel the wind on her face. She told her friend.

"Don't fall off this time."

"No, I won't."

She walked down to the barn and got a bridle from the tack room. Going out into the pasture, she saw Buck. She hadn't ridden him since her fall. She walked up to the horse and slipped the bridle on him. Leading him to the barn, she tied him up while she got the rest of the equipment.

Soon she was in the saddle again. She didn't try to hide her direction this afternoon. She didn't intend to ride more than an hour or two. She wanted time to shower and dress for Jim's return.

She knew it didn't matter how she looked. What mattered was what he was thinking. Whether he was still interested in her.

She was riding by herself, thinking about her

future, when she ran into a group of riders one of the Lazy L cowboys was leading. Joining the group would distract her from her nerves, she reasoned, and that was a good thing.

Two hours later, they were still riding, but several of the riders were lagging. Catching up with the cowboy, she suggested he should take the riders back to the barn. It was an hour and a half later when the barn came into sight.

Jessica had intended to get back earlier. It was already four-thirty and she felt she had to help with the unsaddling. Luckily Hank relieved her.

"I heard Jim would be back for dinner. You don't want to smell like a horse, do you?"

Rather breathlessly, she thanked her brother and headed for a shower. She wanted to be beautiful when Jim came in.

After a shower, she dressed in a denim skirt and a pink blouse. She did her hair in a French braid after she blew it dry. Applying her makeup with a light hand, she surveyed herself in the mirror.

"It will have to work."

She sprayed on her favorite scent and took a deep breath. Going out into the kitchen, she got a thumbs-up sign from Mary Jo.

She smiled in return but didn't stop.

Trying to appear casual, she wandered out to the reception area. She nodded at Leslie, who was there reading a book, then peeked out the window that looked out at the front parking lot. "Where does Jim usually park his car?"

"I thought he usually parked in the front."

Jessica looked again. "I think a car just turned in the drive. It's definitely black. I think it's him!" she said, excitement in her voice.

She suddenly turned and walked into the dining room, wanting to look casual and relaxed when he arrived.

There were already some guests gathering for dinner. Jessica sat down with some of the riders from this afternoon. Trying to hide her concentration on what was happening out front, she discussed riding with them.

When she heard Leslie greet Jim, her heart skipped a beat. Taking a deep breath, she turned her head toward the door. Jim appeared there almost instantly.

"Jim! You're back!"

"Yeah, Jessie, I'm back. Why don't you walk with me to put up my luggage. We can catch up on what I've missed."

"Sure." She jumped up to walk with him, not even noticing what anyone else said.

When they went through the kitchen, he waved to Mary Jo, but he didn't stop. Neither did she. In silence they walked into the back hall.

Once they were out of sight, Jim immediately dropped his bag and wrapped his arms around Jessica. "I missed you," he whispered in her ear.

"I missed you, too. What—what did you find out?" She was almost afraid to ask. But she had to know.

"It wasn't mine."

The words were like a balm to her wounded heart. She let out a deep sigh, the first true exhalation in days.

"At first she didn't know if it was mine," he explained, "because she'd been sleeping with Deke at least a month before I left."

"I'm sorry, Jim."

He nodded. "Deke called me about 4:00 a.m. and told me they were at the hospital and he thought she was having a miscarriage. I went to the hospital and waited with him. When the doctor came out to tell us about the miscarriage, Deke asked whose baby it was. He told us the baby had a B blood type, and I knew that meant the baby was Deke's. I caught a plane as fast as I could."

"How did you know that made the baby Deke's?"

"I'm an A type and Bronwyn is an O. It couldn't be mine."

"I'm sorry she lost the baby."

"Me, too, but I'm very glad it wasn't mine. I knew I'd been responsible." His eyes darkened. "Have you forgiven me?"

"Of course." Almost before the words were out of her mouth, he kissed her.

His arms wrapped around her so tightly she couldn't breathe. But who cared about that? She was where she wanted to be.

"Oh, Jess, I've missed you so much. I need you tonight."

As if on cue, they both heard the gong that meant dinner was served. Though she was hungry for Jim, not dinner, she knew they had to show up in the dining room. Satisfying each other's needs would have to wait. "Drop your bag in your room and let's go eat."

When they got to dinner, there weren't two places together. They both looked at each other and then parted to take the empty seats.

Jessica couldn't remember what she ate. It must've been something she liked, she guessed. Her mind was preoccupied by thoughts of what she and Jim would be doing in just a short while.

After a respectable time she looked for Jim. He'd finished his dessert and was chatting with several people at his table. One of the seats at his table was empty and she left her seat to take the one next to him.

"You finished? That was a great dessert, wasn't it?" Jim asked.

Jessica looked at him blankly. "What?"

"The dessert, the strawberry shortcake."

"Oh. Yes, it was nice." She had no idea if she'd eaten it.

"Do you have to run the bingo tonight?" he whispered.

She shook her head. Leslie had offered to fill in for her.

He cleared his throat and addressed his dinner companions. "Well, it was nice to visit with you tonight. Bingo will be played in here in a few minutes, after they clean away the meal."

Jim got up and pulled Jessica to her feet. He waved goodbye and headed for the back hall, holding Jessica's hand. He didn't stop until he reached his bedroom. "My room tonight, okay?"

"Let me get a robe first."

"Okay, but hurry."

"Are we in a hurry?" she asked.

"No. I just want to make love to you."

"I want that, too."

He was waiting when she knocked on his door. He pulled her into his arms and closed the door with his foot.

Chapter Sixteen

For Jim, all was right with the world the next morning.

He'd spent the night with Jess, making love to her twice and then holding her in his arms all night long. When the alarm went off at six-thirty, his only regret was not having longer with her.

"I've got to get up, honey. Want me to set the alarm for later for you?"

"Uh, yes, please."

"Okay, I'll set it for eight."

With a kiss that he was forced to break off if he was going to get up, he headed for the shower. In no time, he was dressed, shaved and ready for his day.

Cliff was waiting for breakfast when Jim came in. "Howdy, boy. It's good to have you back."

"I'm glad to be back, too."

"Have you heard the news?"

"What news?"

"Leslie agreed to marry me!"

"That's great!" Jim enthused as he shook Cliff's hand.

"We're thinking about building us a house close

by on the ranch so we'd have our own place. That little bedroom I've got wouldn't be big enough for the two of us."

"That sounds nice, but how long will it take to build a house?"

"Maybe three or four months. We've agreed to wait until it's ready before we get married."

"I guess that'll take some patience on your part."

"Yeah, but it'll be that much sweeter if we wait."

"Right," Jim said. But he was thinking about his own situation. Of course, he and Jess weren't waiting. But he didn't want to hide their relationship. If they got engaged, he supposed everyone would accept his sleeping with Jess, but planning a wedding this soon seemed a little rushed.

"Yeah, it's going to be great," Cliff said.

"What?"

"Our marriage. It will be so nice to have someone to share everything. I've been lonely since my wife died."

"Yes, that will be nice."

"I was hoping Jessie would be up so I could tell her, but I guess she's sleeping late. She seemed real out of kilter yesterday. She said she had a headache, but she never has headaches."

"Uh, yeah, I heard that. Maybe a little sleep will help her."

"Yeah, she didn't even come to bingo night. I noticed you weren't there, either."

"I got an early start around 4:00 a.m. yesterday. I was worn out."

"That's pretty early."

"Yeah." Jim was grateful the buffet was set up. He led them over to the table, then they sat down to eat with several guests.

As he ate, he found himself reliving his night with Jess. It was certainly memorable, after his horrendous trip to New York. His hospital visit with Deke had certainly not been a highlight in his life.

Several people departing his table, including Cliff, awoke Jim to what was going on around him. He got up and moved to Pete's table, where there were a couple of chairs vacant now. Sitting down by Pete, Jim asked him how things had gone while he was away.

"Good. Now that we've started working together, with your leadership, I think we're going to be all right."

Jim smiled. "I think so, too. But you're not trying to get rid of me, are you?"

"No," Pete said, smiling. "I think we'll still need you."

"Good, because I'm just settling in."

Pete grinned. "Yeah, I've noticed."

Not sure what Pete was referring to, he just agreed. He didn't think everyone knew about him and Jess. He hoped he wasn't going to have a fight on his hands when her brothers knew about them.

"What are you going to do today?"

"I've been helping Hank with riding lessons.

We've both settled down, learning to deal with our guests. It's going well right now."

"That's great. How about the cattle operation?"

"Andy's doing well. I'm going to be able to ride in a few days. The doctor has promised to put a new cast on me from the knee down. I can ride with that."

"That's great, Pete."

"Yeah."

"Hey, Jim, good to have you back," Hank said. He sat down beside Jim.

"Pete was just telling me he's helping at the corral."

"Yeah, he's doing a good job."

"I'm proud of both of you. You're doing a much better job."

Hank gave him a grin. "Yeah, we're all doing better. And I hear you and Jessie are doing better, too."

"What do you mean?" Pete asked sharply.

"You don't know?" Hank said with a laugh.

"No. What is he talking about?" Pete asked Jim.

Jim didn't want to answer, but he had no choice. Hank was going to tell his brother if Jim didn't. "Jessica and I have been…dating."

"Dating? Hell, I'd call it more than that," Hank said.

Pete sat up straight. "Are you telling me he's sleeping with Jessie?"

Jim tried to quieten their conversation. "Pete, I know you think I'm being hypocritical, but I'm not. The attraction is mutual. Jessie isn't doing anything she doesn't want to do."

Pete leaned across the table, his air menacing.

"Are you telling me what you're doing is all right, but what I did was so horrible?"

Jim stared at Pete. Finally, he answered, "I haven't betrayed your sister as you did Mary Jo."

Hank stared at his brother. "What did you do to Mary Jo?"

"Damn! We're talking about Jessie, not Mary Jo," Pete returned.

"Well, I'm talking about Mary Jo!" Hank argued. "She's a nice lady and does a heck of a job putting good food on the table. Did you mess with her?"

"Yes! I slept with Mary Jo and then with that woman you fixed me up with."

Hank looked disgusted. "Why did you do that to Mary Jo?"

"I didn't think, okay? I regretted it but—but she wouldn't listen to me. Now, can we talk about our sister?"

"Could you lower your voice, Pete?" Jim asked.

"Fine, yeah, I can lower my voice. Now, tell me why it's okay for you to sleep with my sister. Aren't you her boss?"

"Yes, technically, but—"

"Does Granddad know?" Pete continued.

"No, he doesn't."

"And is he going to think it's all right for you to—"

"To what, Pete?" Jessica said, having come to breakfast and heard their discussion.

"You need to have your head examined, little sister!"

"I'm old enough to make my own decisions."

Pete tried to get up with his crutches, but it was a struggle. "I'm your big brother, Jessie. I don't want to hear this."

"Then don't ask questions!" Jessica returned.

"Someone has to take care of you. Dad's not here, so that job falls to me, and I'm ordering you to behave yourself."

Cliff came into the dining room because Leslie hadn't arrived yet. When he saw his family gathered together and indulging in a yelling match, he hurried over.

"What's wrong?"

All of the yelling stopped and they stared at one another. Then Jim said, "I've been romantically involved with Jessie. I intend to ask her to marry me."

To everyone's surprise, Jessica said, "No! I won't marry you." And she ran out of the room.

JIM COULDN'T FIND JESSICA.

After he'd talked to Cliff, he couldn't find out what had happened. He went back to her room, but she didn't answer. He walked to the corral, but she wasn't there. Her horse was.

When he returned to the dining room, he found Leslie with Cliff. Congratulating her on her future marriage, he asked if she'd seen Jessica. She hadn't.

"You'd better find her, boy!" Cliff said. His voice held a threat.

"I'm trying, Cliff. And I was serious about my intentions. But I hadn't told her yet. It was unfortunate that she had to hear it that way."

"I'll be waiting to hear the good news," Cliff retorted.

Jim walked out of the dining room. Where was she? He'd searched everywhere. Clearly she'd found a different place to hide.

JESSICA WAS HIDING IN the last cabin. She knew it was empty, and she didn't think Jim would look for her here.

She'd been humiliated by her brothers this morning. Worst of all, Jim had been forced to offer marriage. It was impossible to accept his proposal when he hadn't really intended to make the offer.

Tears slid down her cheeks, but after a while she'd recovered. Her dreams were shattered. What was she going to do? Leave her home, her job, her life?

There was no acceptable answer. She'd debated any answer until she was totally defeated.

Her car was parked behind the main building. She could reach her car during lunch, when everyone was in the dining room. But where would she go?

And for how long?

Tears rolled down her cheeks again. She felt so totally alone, after being at the height of happiness. It was incredible how quickly her life had changed.

The door to the cabin suddenly opened and Jim walked in. "Jessie, I've been looking for you everywhere."

She turned her back, determined not to face him.

He crossed the room and turned her around. "What are you doing?"

"Nothing!"

"Why did you run away?"

"Oh, please! That's a dumb question."

"Well, here's another dumb question. Why won't you marry me?"

"You know why!" She struggled to remove his hands from her.

"No, I don't. Tell me why, Jessie."

"You didn't bargain on my brothers when you made love to me. And you hadn't mentioned marriage until they confronted you. I don't blame you. It wasn't your fault."

"What wasn't my fault? You're not making sense."

"Yes, I am. I rejected your offer because it wasn't your real intent."

"How do you know that?"

"I'm not an idiot," she said, sadly sniffing away her tears.

"You'd have to be to think I don't love you," Jim said gently, wiping away her tears.

"Sure, and that's why you never mentioned marriage!"

"Hell! We didn't have time to talk about anything! After we made love the first time, Bronwyn told you she was pregnant with my child. The second time we made love, we were both so eager for each other we didn't have any conversation. That's it. That's the sum total of our lovemaking. So how do you know what I was thinking?"

"I know what happened this morning. You were forced to offer marriage to get out of trouble."

"And that's why I've been running around like a crazy man trying to find you?"

She threw up her hands. "Just forget it, Jim. I can't have an affair with you because of my family!"

"I won't argue that with you, Jessie. But I can argue my right to ask you to marry me. Just because we jumped to the marrying part doesn't mean I don't love you." He paced across the room. "Even now I want to touch you so badly it hurts. Let me touch you, Jessie. Let me take you in my arms and kiss you. Let me call you my own."

She bowed her head. Speaking very softly, she said, "I want you to touch me. But I can't let you be forced into marrying me."

"Forced? Come on, Jessie. Were you forced to let me make love to you? Did I take you against your will?"

"No, I wanted you as much as you wanted me."

"Did you want it to be a permanent decision?"

"What are you asking?"

"Did you want to marry me?"

She turned away from him again. "I wanted to see where our relationship took us."

"Me, too. But we weren't given time. And I know I don't want to let you go. I don't think I want to let you go ever again."

"How can you know that?" she questioned, turning to look at him.

"Come here, and I'll show you."

"Jim, I can't—" She broke off her protest because he'd pulled her into his arms and kissed her.

"I can, Jess. I truly can love you the rest of our lives. That's what I know. I know I love you. I know I'll never let you go."

He kissed her again.

And again.

When she finally was allowed to say anything, she could only say, "I love you, too."

"That's what I wanted to hear, Jess. I'm where I want to live, with the one person I want to live with. Forever and ever."

JIM AND JESSICA FACED HER family together, hand in hand.

"We want to get married at once," Jim said, "but we know we can't get away right now. What should we do?"

"You're really going to get married?" Pete asked.

"Yeah, we really are, aren't we, sweetheart?"

"Yes," Jessica said, smiling at Jim.

"So do you want to get married here on the ranch?" Hank asked. "That's what Mom and Dad would've wanted."

"Yeah, but we don't want to wait until the season is over."

"How about Sunday afternoon?" Pete suggested.

"We have a window of about two hours. We could make it at one o'clock and you could go to a hotel in Steamboat Springs for the night. I know it wouldn't be wonderful, but it would make the marriage possible and you could have a honeymoon in October."

Jim turned to Jess. "We could do that."

"That would be great." Jessica smiled at him.

"Then, will you help us have a wedding?"

"Sure, we'll do what we can," Hank said. "And congratulations!"

ON SUNDAY MORNING, JESSICA had breakfast in the kitchen with Mary Jo, who was to be her maid of honor later that day.

"Are you nervous?" Mary Jo asked.

"No. I'm so in love. I know it will last forever." Jessica smiled, thinking about her wedding.

"You'd better eat. We've got things to do."

"Oh, yes," Jessica said with a dreamy smile.

After breakfast, Mary Jo gave Jessica a manicure, then rolled her hair on big rollers.

Sitting under a hair dryer, Jessica felt like a princess. Her nails were a rosy-pink and she had put cream on her face after her shower. Then she sprayed herself with her perfume.

Used to wearing jeans every day, she pulled on hose and a half-slip. Then it was time to put on the outfit that she and Mary Jo had bought on Wednesday. A cream suit that she'd spent a lot of money on.

She checked her appearance in her mirror. "Do you think I look all right?" she asked Mary Jo.

"I think you look gorgeous. The suit makes your dark hair look great and your skin flawless."

"I hope Jim likes it."

"He will, Jessica, I promise you."

Jessica drew a deep breath. "I think I'm ready, then."

"I'll go check and see if they're all set."

It was one o'clock. The pastor from their church had promised he'd be there.

Mary Jo came back into Jessica's bedroom.

"They're all ready for you."

Leslie was waiting for them at the entrance to the living room. She handed Mary Jo a bouquet of pink rosebuds. Then she gave Jessica a larger bouquet with a mixture of white flowers and red rosebuds.

"Now I'm going to start the music."

Much to Jessica's surprise, the wedding march began playing.

Mary Jo went down the length of the living room. She stepped to the left side of the altar formed by a trellis of beautiful flowers.

Jessica blinked rapidly to dispel the tears that formed when she saw the beautiful flowers. Her family had done so much for today to be memorable.

Leslie nudged Jessica. "It's time."

Jessica stepped forward and began walking down the room, her eyes fixed on Jim. They had decided not to sleep together until after their marriage, to make their wedding night more special. Right now she wanted to throw herself at him. Instead, she walked sedately down the room.

His eyes lit up when he saw her. That told her all she needed to know. He loved her, as she loved him.

When she reached him, she smiled.

The pastor asked who gave this woman, and Cliff stood. "Her family gives her to this man."

Hank was Jim's best man because Pete was on crutches. He handed Jim the wedding ring, as did Mary Jo, exchanging the ring for Jessica's bouquet.

When the ceremony ended, Jim took Jessica in his arms and kissed her.

Afterward, they cut the beautiful wedding cake Mary Jo had baked. Jim fed Jessica a bite of cake and then she fed him. The sweetness of the cake was nothing compared to the sweetness of their lives at that moment.

Then they headed to Steamboat Springs for a night of bliss in their hotel.

The rest of the family, including Leslie, celebrated the wedding for hours afterward. Cliff squeezed Leslie's hand and said, "Soon, Leslie and I will marry, too. It's going to be great."

"So you're going to abandon us, too, Granddad?" Pete asked.

"Yes, Leslie has promised to marry me. But don't worry, boys. I'll find you wives, too. Just wait and see."

* * * * *

Mills & Boon® Special Edition
brings you a sneak preview of Christine Rimmer's
In Bed with the Boss,
which is available in May 2009.

*Little did hotel-chain CFO Tom Holloway realise
that his new executive assistant spelled trouble.
But even though single mum Shelly Winston was
planted by Holloway's worst enemy to take him
down, Shelly was no fool – she had a mind of her
own and an eye for her handsome boss!*

*Don't miss this exciting new story coming next
month from Mills & Boon® Special Edition!*

In Bed with the Boss

by

Christine Rimmer

Two years ago...

It was *the* moment.

And Tom Holloway knew it.

Across the black granite boardroom table, Helen Taka-Hanson waited, her beautiful face composed, showing him nothing. Behind her, beyond the floor-to-ceiling windows, the afternoon sun reflected off the tall buildings of North Michigan Avenue. Tom kept his gaze level, on Helen. But he knew what was out there: The Second City. The Magnificent Mile.

Chicago. Tom wanted it. *Needed* it, really. A fresh start in a new town. He would be chief financial officer of TAKA-Hanson's new hospitality division.

Which meant hotels. Contemporary luxury hotels on a grand scale. It was the biggest venture he'd tackled so far and it sounded good. Better than good.

And the job was his. Helen had already made the offer.

What he said next could blow it for him—more than likely *would* blow it for him. Which was why he'd left the crucial information off his résumé. His disgrace had happened so long ago, it was easily glossed over now.

But Tom had learned the hard way that concealment didn't work in the long term. The high-stakes world of finance was too damn small. In the end, his past always found him.

Better to show his stuff first, let them know he had the chops, get all the way to the job offer. And then take a deep breath and lay the bad news right out there.

The offer just might stand in spite of his past. If it didn't, if he lost the job, well, chances were he would have lost it anyway in the end, when the ugly facts surfaced.

Oh, yeah. A delicate moment, this. The moment of truth.

Helen said, "Well, Tom. You've heard our offer. Is there anything else we need to go over?"

Tom sat back in the chair, ordered his body to relax and told himself—for the hundredth time—that it had to be done.

"As a matter of fact, Helen. There is something else…"

She arched a brow at him and waited for him to go on.

He said, "I was fired once. It was a long time ago, my first job out of Princeton."

"Fired." Helen spoke the word flatly. "That's not on your résumé, is it?"

"No. And it gets worse."

"I'm listening."

"I was young and way too hungry, working on Wall Street, determined to make it big and do it fast. None of which is any justification for my actions. I was discharged for insider trading. And then I was arrested for it. And convicted. I did six months."

A silence. A pretty long one. Tom could feel yet another great job slipping away from him.

At last, Helen asked the big question. "Were you guilty?"

"Yes. I was."

He might have softened the harsh fact a little. He could have explained what a naive idiot he'd been then. He could have told her all about his mentor at the time, who'd convinced him to pass certain "tips" to big clients. He could have said that the guy got away clean by setting Tom up to take the fall for him. That the same former mentor had been a curse on his life since then. Because of that one man, Tom had lost out on a number of opportunities—and not just in terms of his career. It would have been the truth.

However, his former boss wasn't the one up for CFO, TAKA-Hanson, hospitality division. Tom was. His prospective employer needed to know that he'd once broken the law—and then gone to jail for it. The why and the wherefore?

Not the question.

Tom sat unflinching, waiting for the ax to fall.

Instead, Helen smiled.

It was a slow smile, and absolutely genuine—a warm smile, the kind of smile that would make any red-blooded man sit up and take notice. From what Tom had heard, this genius of the business world, now in her late forties, had saved Hanson Media from collapse several years back, after her first husband, George Hanson, died suddenly. The story went that before she was forced to step in and save the family business, she'd been a trophy wife.

Smart and savvy and strictly professional as she'd been since he met her, Tom had been having trouble seeing her as mere arm candy for a tycoon. But now he'd been granted that amazing smile, he wasn't having trouble anymore.

That face, that smile…

George Hanson had been one lucky man. And so was her current husband, TAKA-Hanson's chairman of the board, Morito Taka.

"I prize honesty," Helen said. "I prize it highly. So I think it's time I repaid your truth with one of my own. I've done my homework on you, Tom. I've known all along about how you lost that trading job, and the price you paid for what you did. I've been interested to see if you'd tell me about it. And now that you have, I'm more certain than ever on this. Other than that one admittedly serious black mark against you—for which you've paid your dues—your record is spotless. I know you'll make a fine addition to my team. I've got no res-ervations. You're the man for this job."

Tom's heart slammed against his breastbone. Had he

heard right? Had it worked out, after all? The CEO knew the truth.

And she'd hired him anyway.

He held out his hand. Helen took it. They shook.

When he spoke, his voice was firm and level. "I intend to make sure you never regret this decision."

"I believe you," said Helen. "That's another reason you're our new CFO."

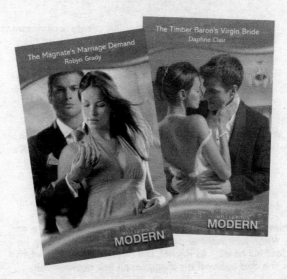

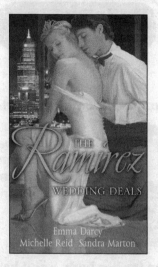

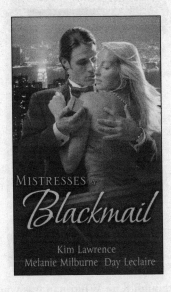

2 FREE

BOOKS AND A SURPRISE GIFT!

We would like to take this opportunity to thank you for reading this Mills & Boon® book by offering you the chance to take TWO more specially selected titles from the Special Edition series absolutely FREE! We're also making this offer to introduce you to the benefits of the Mills & Boon® Book Club™—

★ **FREE home delivery**
★ **FREE gifts and competitions**
★ **FREE monthly Newsletter**
★ **Exclusive Mills & Boon Book Club offers**
★ **Books available before they're in the shops**

Accepting these FREE books and gift places you under no obligation to buy, you may cancel at any time, even after receiving your free shipment. Simply complete your details below and return the entire page to the address below. You don't even need a stamp!

YES! Please send me 2 free Special Edition books and a surprise gift. I understand that unless you hear from me, I will receive 4 superb new titles every month for just £3.19 each, postage and packing free. I am under no obligation to purchase any books and may cancel my subscription at any time. The free books and gift will be mine to keep in any case.

E9ZED

Ms/Mrs/Miss/Mr ....Initials ....

BLOCK CAPITALS PLEASE

Surname ....

Address ....

....

....Postcode..............................

Send this whole page to:
UK: FREEPOST CN81, Croydon, CR9 3WZ